Enemies To Expecting

Mia Caldwell and Mylia Ashton

Published by Mia Caldwell, 2023.

Blurb

She's having her best friend's baby. He's the billionaire she can't stand. Tragedy turns foes into expectant parents.

WHEN JESSICA MALONE agreed to carry her best friend's baby, she never expected Anya and her husband to die in a car accident. That's shocking, but it's even more shocking when she learns the biological father is Holt's best friend, Maddox Tillman. She's never liked Maddox, seeing him as a spoiled and controlling billionaire. Maddox has always considered her a sanctimonious brat with a chip on her shoulder against wealth and privilege.

As the pregnancy progresses, they find themselves drawn to each other despite their differences and mutual dislike. Things are more complicated when Lara, Maddox's long-time girlfriend and a successful PR executive, isn't happy with the situation and isn't willing to accept the child as her own. As they bond over preparing for their daughter's arrival, attraction grows into love, but family opposition and the specter of Maddox's socialite girlfriend threaten their blossoming relationship. Can Jessica and Maddox put aside their prejudices to become the parents their child deserves?

Chapter 1—Jessica

WHEN I ARRIVE FOR BRUNCH, Anya greets me at the door and pulls me into a hug. "How are you feeling?" she asks, rubbing my belly.

"I'm okay. The morning sickness has finally started to subside." I smile at her, glad I've been able to help my best friend have a baby. "It's worth it though."

"I know," she says, her eyes shining. "I can't wait to be a mom."

"You're going to be an amazing mom." I pat her arm reassuringly before following her into the house. She leads me to the kitchen, where Holt is cooking up a storm.

"Hey, Jess." He gives me a quick hug. "How's my little girl doing?"

"She's fine." I chuckle as he kisses my belly before returning to the stove. "I think she's enjoying all the attention."

"Good. You're looking great."

"Thanks." I grin at him, knowing he's only saying it to be polite. I feel like a beached whale, but I'm trying to ignore it. I'm only four months, but I already feel huge.

Anya hands me a glass of water, and we sit down at the table. I glance around, noticing four place settings. I frown at her, wondering who else is coming.

"Don't worry." She laughs. "It's just Maddox."

"Oh, joy." I roll my eyes. "Why did you invite him?"

"Because he's Holt's best friend, and he's a good guy once you get to know him." She raises an eyebrow at me. "I know you two don't see eye-to-eye, but you need to be civil."

"Fine." I sigh, knowing I can't argue with her. "I'll be nice."

We chat for a few minutes until the front door opens, and Maddox walks in. He's dressed casually in jeans and a t-shirt, and his hair is mussed. He looks like he just rolled out of bed, and it annoys me that he can look so effortlessly hot.

"Hey, man." Holt claps him on the back, and they exchange a bro hug. "Glad you could make it."

"Me too." Maddox grins at him before glancing at me. "Hi, Jessica."

"Hi, Maddox." I give him a tight smile, trying to keep my annoyance in check. There's just something about him that sets me on edge.

"How are you feeling?" he asks, nodding at my stomach.

"Fine." I shrug, not wanting to admit that I'm starting to feel uncomfortable. "Just a bit tired."

"That's normal." He sits down next to me and leans forward. "Have you been taking your vitamins?"

"Yes." I narrow my eyes at him. "What do you care?"

"I care about my friends' kid." He shrugs. "I want to make sure you're taking care of yourself."

"I am." I glare at him, irritated by his concern.

"Okay." He holds up his hands. "I was just asking."

"Well, you don't need to." I turn away, ignoring him.

"Sorry about that," Anya whispers to him.

"It's fine." He shakes his head. "I shouldn't have pushed."

"No, you shouldn't." I glare at him again. "Stop acting like you know everything."

"I wasn't." He sighs. "I was just concerned."

I realize there's a chance my hormones and not sleeping well are making me, well...bitchy, so I take a deep breath. "I'm sorry. I shouldn't have snapped at you for asking about Holt and Anya's baby. I'm a bit tired, and my back hurts."

"It's okay." He smiles at me. "I think what you're doing for our friends is amazing. Do you have any weird cravings yet?"

"Not yet." I laugh. "I'm sure I will soon. I hear that's common with pregnancy."

"Yeah." He chuckles. "I remember when my cousin was pregnant. She was eating pickles and peanut butter."

"That sounds gross." I wrinkle my nose. "I hope I don't get that."

"I'm sure you won't." He winks at me. "You seem like you have good taste."

"I do." I smile at him, realizing he's actually kind of charming. Maybe he's not as bad as I thought.

Holt announces that breakfast is ready, and we all pile food onto our plates. I eat slowly, savoring every bite. I need to eat healthy, but I also want to enjoy my favorite foods while I can. I already miss coffee so much, but Anya is like a sister, so this baby is my niece. I'm going to do everything I can to keep her healthy.

"This is delicious." I moan as I take another bite of bacon. "I might have to come over here every day."

"I wish you would." Holt beams at me. "I love cooking for people."

"I know you do." I grin at him. "I bet you were a chef in a past life."

"Maybe." He laughs, looking wistful for a second. "Who knows? It sounds better than being a corporate drone."

I snort. "You're hardly a drone. You're heir to your company and a future billionaire." I try not to let my disdain show in the last word.

"True." He nods. "I'd still rather cook than deal with board meetings and investors all day."

"Fair point." I nod. "I guess we all have our passions."

"Exactly." He points at me. "And yours is helping others have babies."

I laugh. "I guess that's true since I've worked on the OB floor for a while. I just never expected to go from nurse to surrogate."

"I'm glad you did though." Anya squeezes my hand. "You're the only one I trust with this baby."

"Thank you." I squeeze her hand back. "You know I'll do anything for you and Holt."

"I know." She smiles at me. "Which is why I love you so much."

"Love you too." I lean over and kiss her cheek. "Now, let's finish this delicious meal and then watch some trashy TV while Holt cleans up."

"Deal." She grins at me. "Let's do it."

"Hey!" Holt protests. "I cooked. Someone else should clean."

I laugh. "You have a point." I glance at Maddox. "Want to help him?"

"Sure." He nods. "I'll rinse the dishes."

I blink. "You know how to do dishes?"

"Of course." He rolls his eyes. "I'm not a complete idiot."

"I didn't mean..." I trail off, realizing I'm being rude again. "Sorry. I just assumed you had staff to do that sort of thing."

"I do, but I also know how to take care of myself." He shrugs. "My housekeeper gets the weekend off, so I have to fend for myself."

"Oh." I stare at him, realizing there's more to him than I realized. "That's...good."

"Thanks." He smirks at me. "I appreciate your approval."

"Whatever." I roll my eyes and return to my plate, accidentally noticing once again how damned hot he is. It's unfair. The last thing I need is to be attracted to Maddox Tillman. That would be a disaster because I dislike what he stands for, and he has a long-time girlfriend. Laura or Lara? I don't remember which.

After breakfast, we settle in the living room and watch some trashy reality shows. I have to admit it's fun, and I'm laughing harder than I have in a long time. Maddox is funny and sarcastic, and I find myself liking trading barbs with him. It's a strange shift from hating him to tolerating him, but I'm trying to embrace it.

As the afternoon wears on, I realize I'm getting sleepy. I stifle a yawn, and Maddox glances at me. "Are you okay?"

"Yeah." I nod. "Just tired. I didn't sleep well last night."

"Do you want to lie down?" He gestures toward the couch. "There's plenty of room." He pauses. "Unless you want to go home?"

"No, it's okay." I shake my head, not wanting to leave yet. "I'll just rest my eyes for a few minutes."

"Okay." He nods. "If you need anything, let me know."

I'm surprised by his offer because it seems sincere. I move over to the large chaise that's part of the sectional beside Maddox and curl up on my side. It's comfortable, and I close my eyes, letting the sound of the TV lull me to sleep.

When I wake up, it's late afternoon, and I realize I've been asleep for a couple of hours. My head is lying on something hard and warm, and I blink up in surprise to see Maddox glancing down at me. "Did I fall asleep on your leg?"

"Yeah." He chuckles. "You looked so peaceful that I didn't want to disturb you."

"Oh, god." I sit up quickly. "I'm sorry." Heat creeps up my cheeks as I realize I was practically using him as a pillow, and it was probably very uncomfortable for him. I slept like the dead, so I apparently found lying on him way too comfortable.

I blush harder, thankful my darker skin hides that as I scramble up. It had to be exhaustion and the fact that his body was warm and inviting. It's not like I'm attracted to him or anything. "I'm sorry," I repeat. "I didn't mean to fall asleep on you."

"It's okay." He shrugs. "You seemed tired, and I didn't mind. It gave me a chance to catch up on the news." He gestures to the tablet in his lap.

"Oh." I blink at him. "You didn't have to stay."

"I wanted to." He smiles at me. "I like spending time with my friends, even if they are surly sometimes." He winks at me.

"Sorry." I grimace. "I think it's the pregnancy hormones."

"You haven't liked me since we met, and you haven't been pregnant for eight years." There's a note of teasing in his voice, but his eyes seem serious, like he's bothered by the animosity between us.

"I know." I sigh. "I just don't like the idea of money buying things that other people can't afford."

"That's fair." He nods. "But not everyone with money is evil, you know."

"I know, but it's hard to separate the good guys from the assholes when you're poor." I shrug. "I'm sorry if I've been rude to you. It's not personal."

"It's okay. I understand." He smiles at me again. "Maybe we can make more of an effort. I know it'd make Anya and Holt happy if we could be friendly, especially with the baby coming. I'm sure we'll both be here a lot helping out."

My eyes widen. "You plan to help out with the baby?" I can't picture it. He was born with a silver spoon in every orifice, just like Holt. I'm frankly amazed he hasn't suggested they hire a nanny.

"Of course." He blinks at me. "I'm going to be her uncle, so I want to be involved."

"Oh." I stare at him, realizing there's more depth to him than I thought. "That's...sweet." Trying to make conversation, I ask, "Are you and Laura planning a family?"

"Lara," he says with a brief smile. "And no, we aren't. She doesn't like kids, and I don't want any of my own."

"Really?" I blink at him. "Don't you have some obligation to pass on your legacy, or some billionaire thing like that? I mean, you're the vice president of your father's company, right?"

"Yes, but I'm not a fan of nepotism, and I'm not a fan of children." He shrugs. "I'm happy to be an uncle, but I don't want the responsibility of raising one. I'm not cut out for it."

"Wow." I stare at him, trying to reconcile this new information with what I know of him. "It's good you know that before having kids." I think about foster care for a minute but quickly try to block out that bleak time in my life. It was misery, but at least I met Anya, so something amazing came from it.

"Yeah." He nods. "I don't want to waste anyone's time. I know I'm not father material, and Lara agrees. She doesn't want to be a mom either."

"Huh." I frown. "She sounds like the perfect wife for you, with her socialite background and ambition."

"She will be when we get around to making it official, I guess." He shrugs. "We both have our own goals and ambitions, and neither of us wants to compromise on them. Our parents will object, but that's their problem, not hers and mine. We can make our own choices."

"Good for you." I smile at him. "You should be able to live your life the way you want to."

"Thanks." He smiles back. "So, are we good now?" He holds out his hand. "Friends?"

"Yeah, friends." I take his hand and shake it, feeling a spark of electricity shoot through me. I ignore it, knowing it's just a fluke. It's not like I'm attracted to Maddox Tillman. That would be ridiculous.

"Where are Anya and Holt?" I just realized they aren't with us.

"In the nursery. They're painting, so you aren't allowed up there, per Anya's orders. Holt asked me to keep you entertained if you woke before they finished. Apparently, you're a terrible artist."

"Ha-ha." I roll my eyes. "I prefer to focus on my medical skills, not my artistic ones."

"I can respect that." He nods. "I'm not much of an artist either. I can play the piano, but that's about it."

"Really?" I blink at him. "I didn't know that." I pause. "I'm a terrible dancer, but I love to dance."

"I can teach you." He grins. "I've been told I'm a great teacher."

"I bet you are." I smile back. "I'll take you up on that sometime." I stretch. "They have a piano in the library. Will you play for me? You have to keep me entertained like I'm a child, after all," I say with a twinge of annoyance at Holt but mostly good-naturedly.

"Sure." He nods. "Follow me."

He leads me into the library, where a beautiful grand piano sits in the corner. I don't know why Holt and Anya have it since neither of them plays. They must have bought it for the aesthetic. I sit down on the bench and gesture for him to join me. He slides in beside me and starts playing a classical piece. His fingers fly over the keys, and I'm mesmerized.

"You're really good," I say, my eyes wide. "You didn't tell me you were this good."

"It's just a hobby." He shrugs. "I'm not a professional or anything."

"Still, you have talent." I smile at him, feeling a warmth spread through me, and it's not just from the music.

"Thanks." He smiles back, and I feel that same spark from earlier. Ignoring it, I focus on the music, letting it wash over me.

After he finishes the song, he turns to me. "Would you like me to teach you?"

"Sure." I nod. "I want to. There were no opportunities in foster care, and I haven't had the time as an adult. I always wanted to learn though."

"I'll teach you." He smiles at me. "We can start with scales and work up to songs."

"Sounds good." I grin back. "I'm excited."

"Me too." He winks at me. "Let's get started."

As he begins to teach me, I realize I'm having a great time. Maddox is patient and encouraging, and I find myself relaxing and enjoying the lesson. By the time we stop, I'm exhausted and starving.

"I think I need some dinner." I glance at the doorway. "I doubt it's taking them this long to paint."

He chuckles. "They probably sneaked away for a quickie. They can't keep their hands off each other."

"That's a good thing after being together eight years," I say with a sigh of envy. "I wish I could have that."

"You will." He pats my shoulder. "You're a gorgeous woman. You'll find someone who adores you."

"I hope so." I sigh. "It's just hard when you're a nurse and don't have time to date." I pause. "I haven't dated in a long time. I'm not sure I even remember how."

"You'll be fine." He smiles at me. "You're witty and smart. Any guy would be lucky to have you."

"Thanks." Things feel awkward for a moment, so it's a relief when Anya and Holt appear.

"There you are. We were looking for you," says Anya.

I grin, noticing her top is buttoned wrong. "I'm sure you were looking *hard*."

She blushes and adjusts her shirt. "We were painting."

"Uh-huh." I smirk at her. "Maddox was teaching me to play the piano. He's quite talented."

"I know." She nods. "He's full of surprises."

"Indeed." I glance at him, wondering what else he's hiding.

"Anyway, Holt and I are going to order pizza. What kind do you want?" asks Anya.

"Pepperoni, please." I smile at her. "I'm starving."

"Me too." She grins. "Pregnancy does that to you." Her expression dims for a moment, and I know she's thinking about the three babies she lost before accepting she'll never be able to carry to term.

I get up from the bench and go hug her. "It's okay. You're going to be a great mom to this baby, and you'll be there for her every step of the way."

"I know." She sniffles. "I'm just grateful I have you."

"Always." I hold her tightly, knowing she's the sister I always wished for even if there's no DNA between us. We're both sniffling when I pull away. "Pepperoni and mushrooms." I clear my throat, and she does the same.

Holt is already putting in the order with his phone.

"So...what are you going to name the kid?" asks Maddox, clearly trying to fill the silence.

"It's a girl," says Anya. "We're going to name her Charlotte."

Holt frowns. "Or Piper."

Maddox looks at me. "Are you far enough along to know that?"

I shake my head. "No. It's just a feeling Anya has. She's always been intuitive."

"It's definitely a girl," says Anya. "Just wait and see." She smiles at me. "Jessica, do you want to come with me to the baby store tomorrow? We need to buy a crib and changing table, among other things."

"Sure." I nod. "You know you have plenty of time though, right? The baby isn't due for another five months."

"I know." She sighs. "I just want to be prepared."

"I get it." I pat her arm. "I'm here for you, and I'll help you with whatever you need."

"I know." She gives me a watery smile. "You've always been there for me."

"And I always will be." I smile back. "Now, let's eat. I'm famished."

Chapter 2—Maddox

I LET MYSELF INTO MY apartment late that evening, having spent longer than I'd planned with my best friends...and Jessica. I'm disconcerted by how much she's on my mind. It must be because she's practically glowing with her pregnancy.

That, and she actually warmed up a bit today. She's a nice person, and I like her. I like her a lot, and I don't know what to do about it. She's my best friend's surrogate, and she hates me. Or at least she did. I'm not sure anymore. She was nicer to me today and even smiled at me a few times. After eight years, I feel like we're making progress.

Lara is on the couch, wearing cucumber slices on her eyes, with her feet soaking in a tub thing that bubbles. I press a kiss to her head, not wanting that gunk on her face on my lips. I know it's gross from experience. "Tough day?" I ask. She couldn't make it to brunch because she was putting out a PR fire for her biggest client, some rockstar named Felipe Morney, who, according to her, has more money than sense.

"You have no idea." She groans. "I swear, that man is going to be the death of me. He can't stay out of trouble for more than two days."

"What happened this time?" I sit down beside her and remove my shoes and socks, sticking my feet in the bubbling water next to hers. It feels amazing, and I lean back against the cushion with a sigh.

"He got arrested for public intoxication and resisting arrest." She sighs. "I had to bail him out and convince the judge to drop the charges."

"How much is his bail?" I ask, curious.

"Five thousand." She removes the cucumbers from her eyes and tosses them in the bowl on the coffee table. "I'm charging him double my usual rate."

"That's fair." I nod. "You're worth every penny."

"Damn straight." She smirks at me. "Especially since I have to deal with his nonsense."

"True." I chuckle. "You're a saint."

"I know." She smiles at me. "How was your day with Anya and Holt?"

"It was good." I nod. "They're excited about the baby."

"I bet." She smiles. "I'm glad they finally found a surrogate. I know they've been struggling to conceive."

"Yeah, Jessica is a good friend. She's doing them a huge favor." I lean back and close my eyes, enjoying the heat from the water.

"Jessica?" Lara sounds confused. "Who's Jessica?"

"Anya's best friend." I open one eye to look at her. "She's their surrogate. You met her at their wedding."

"Oh, right." She nods. "The dark-skinned woman, right?"

"Yes, that's her." I wince, not liking how she describes her.

"She seems nice." Lara shrugs. "I didn't talk to her much, but she seemed pleasant enough."

"She is to everyone but me." I whisper. "She doesn't care for me."

Lara's eyes widen comically. "Impossible. No woman alive can resist you. You're the most desirable man in the city."

"Apparently not." I shrug. "She's always been cool to me, and I don't know why."

"Maybe she's jealous of your money." She waves her hand dismissively. "Some women are like that." Like me, she comes from a privileged background, so she clearly can't relate. I can't either, at least not entirely, but I've debated Jessica enough times to know she has a chip on her shoulder about wealth, but she's not wrong about how it's often frivolously used.

"Maybe." I shrug. "I'm not sure."

"Maybe you should ask her." She leans over and kisses my cheek. "You're the best boyfriend ever, and I'm glad she doesn't like you. I don't have to worry about anyone stealing you away." She smiles, and the words are just what she should say, but I get the feeling she's just saying them.

It's been like that a lot between us for the last several months. I'm worried we're drifting apart, but I haven't had the courage to broach the subject. I tell myself we're both just busy, but...it feels like more than that.

"I'm sorry I missed brunch." She rests her head on my shoulder. "I'll make it up to you."

"It's okay." I shrug. "I had fun."

"Good." She snuggles closer to me. "I'm glad."

We sit in silence for a while, and it's nice. As the hour grows later, I'm disappointed but not surprised when she stands up, stretching.

"I'm going to call it a night. I have to be up early to put out Felipe's fires." She yawns. "I'll probably fall asleep the minute my head hits the pillow, so I'll see you in the morning."

In other words, no intimacy again. I nod, not protesting. I miss the connection we used to have more than the sex, but I'm not inclined to try to convince her. If she doesn't want me, I won't force her. I've never been that kind of guy, and I'm not starting now.

"Okay." I stand up, kissing her hair to avoid the goop. "Sleep well."

"You too." She smiles at me, but it doesn't reach her eyes. I watch her walk away, wondering if I should say something, but I let her go.

I sit back down and finish soaking my feet, but I'm restless. I decide to take a shower and then read for a while, but I can't concentrate. I keep thinking about Jessica and how much I enjoyed spending time with her. I like her a lot more than I should, and I'm worried I might be developing feelings for her.

I'm not sure what to do about that, since she's made it clear she dislikes me, and I'm unofficially engaged to Lara. She doesn't wear my ring, and I haven't asked her, but we've discussed our wedding venue, how many people to invite, and all the rest. It feels like it's settled.

But am I settling? Is Lara the person I want to spend the rest of my life with? I'm not sure anymore, and that scares me. I'm not sure what to do about any of it, so I push aside my thoughts and go to bed. Lara, wearing a sleep mask, is already snoring softly as I slide into my side. There's a vast swath of emptiness between us, but I don't try to cross it. Instead, I lie there staring at the ceiling until I drift off to sleep.

WHEN I WAKE UP THE next morning, Lara is already gone, and I'm not surprised. She's always the first one out of bed, and she's usually gone before I even open my eyes. I check my email and text messages, and I see a message from Jessica.

"Hey, thanks for the piano lessons yesterday. I had a great time."

I smile as I type a reply. *"You're welcome. I had a great time too. Maybe I can teach you more sometime."*

She responds quickly. *"I'd like that. I'll be at Anya and Holt's this weekend, like usual."*

My heart skips a beat. *"Great. I'll see you then."*

I can't stop smiling as I get ready for work. I'm looking forward to seeing Jessica this weekend, and I'm not sure what to make of that. I shouldn't be developing feelings for her, especially when I'm technically engaged to Lara, but I can't seem to help myself. There's just something about Jessica that draws me to her, and I can't resist.

Truthfully, I've always felt a certain pull to her, and I love trading barbs with her, or I did. Now that she's pregnant, my inclination is to be gentler with her. I want to protect her, and I want to be a part of her life, and that scares me. I'm not sure what to do about these growing feelings, but I need to figure it out soon. Otherwise, someone could get hurt, and it could be me.

I'm distracted at work, and I end up leaving early to grab a drink with Holt. I meet him at a bar near his office, and he's already there, nursing a beer.

"Hey, man, what's up?" He claps me on the back as I sit down across from him.

"Not much." I shrug. "Just a long day at the office."

"Tell me about it." He shakes his head. "I had to deal with a client who wanted to sue a company for having an employee who wore a T-shirt with a logo on it."

"Seriously?" I raise an eyebrow. "Were they suing the company or the employee?"

"The company." He rolls his eyes. "Can you believe that?"

"Actually, yes." I laugh. "People will sue over anything these days. I'm glad I'm not swimming in corporate law waters alongside you, my friend."

"Yeah, me, too." He sighs. "It's exhausting sometimes and full of sharks, and I don't even have to go to court. I just handle the admin side, but I still see a lot of crazy at Dad's firm. Some working right beside me." He shudders, looking pensive. "I've been thinking about telling Dad to chuck it all."

I blink. "Huh? Can we do that?" I joke.

He smiles but slowly nods. "Anya totally supports me. I want to..." He seems embarrassed. "I want to open a restaurant once Charlotte's born, and we have down our routine. She's supportive of it, and I think we can make it work."

"Wow." I stare at him. "That's a big change."

"It is." He nods. "But it's something I've been thinking about for a long time." He manages a half-smile. "My dad's gonna freak."

I take a sip of my whiskey. "I take it this is more than just casual talking then?"

"Yeah." He nods. "I'm serious about it. I'm going to give notice after the baby's born."

"I support you." I smile at him. "If you're happy, I'm happy." I laugh. "I don't envy you telling your folks though. I imagine they'll take it about as well as mine if I told them I'm doing something completely different. It's one of the reasons I've stuck with the family business."

"You could quit, you know," he says, frowning. "You don't have to follow in your father's footsteps."

"I know." I sip my drink. "I just haven't found the right path yet. I'm still searching, I guess."

"You'll find it." He claps me on the shoulder. "You're a smart guy. You'll figure it out."

"Thanks." I smile at him. "So, are you nervous about the baby?"

"Nah." He shrugs. "I mean, I'm a little anxious, but I know we'll be fine. We'll figure it out together, like we always do."

"That's true." I nod. "We're a team."

He bumps my shoulder. "I meant me and Anya, but we couldn't do this without you." His expression turns somber. "You're the best, man."

"You too." I smile at him. "I'm honored to be a part of this journey with you and Anya. It means a lot to me."

"It means a lot to us too." He grins. "Now, enough of the mushy stuff. Let's get drunk and talk about sports."

"Sounds suitably manly. Count me in." I laugh.

We spend the rest of the evening drinking and talking, and I'm glad to have such a good friend. Holt has always been there for me, and I know he always will be. It's a comforting thought, and I'm grateful to have him in my life. We're both only children, but in each other, we've found brothers.

As the night wears on, I find myself thinking about Jessica and wondering if she's okay. I hope she's taking care of herself, and I make a mental note to ask her about it when I see her this weekend. I'm looking forward to it more than I should, but I can't help it. There's just something about her that draws me in, and I can't resist.

"Hey, man, you okay?" Holt asks, snapping his fingers in front of my face. "You look like you're a million miles away."

"Sorry, just thinking about work." I lie, not wanting to admit I'm thinking about Jessica. "And...Lara." I add, hoping he'll buy it.

"Ah, yeah, how're things with you two?" He raises an eyebrow. "You guys getting hitched anytime soon?"

"I don't know." I shrug. "Things have been kind of weird lately. Neither of us have brought it up, but I feel like we're drifting apart."

"Really?" He frowns. "I'm sorry, man. That sucks."

"Yeah, it does." I sigh. "I'm not sure what to do about it. On the one hand, I love her and want to make things work, but on the other hand, I'm not sure if she's the right person for me. Does that make sense?"

"Sure." He nods. "Sometimes, you just have to follow your gut. If you're not sure, you should probably call it off. I don't want to see you miserable, and neither would Lara, I'm sure."

"I know." I sigh. "I just don't want to hurt her. She's a good person, and I care about her. I love her, but I'm not sure I'm *in* love with her. We grew up together, and we drifted together. It felt natural, but there's no spark, you know?" My shoulders slump as I think of Jessica. "I feel like I could have that with someone else, but I'm not sure if she's interested."

"Who?" He looks at me, curious. "Anyone I know?"

"Just a girl I met through Anya and Holt."

Holt grins. "I'm Holt." Then his eyes widen, and he's not so drunk that he doesn't grasp who I mean. "Holy crap, man. She hates you."

"I know." I groan. "I can't help it though. There's something about her that draws me in, and I can't resist. She's smart, funny, and beautiful. She's also a great person and cares deeply about her friends and family. How can I not be attracted to her?"

"Dude." He stares at me. "This is a mess. What are you going to do?"

"I have no idea." I shake my head. "I'm not sure what to do, but I need to figure it out soon. This isn't fair to Lara, and I don't want to hurt her."

"I know." He squeezes my shoulder. "You're a good guy, Maddox. Whatever you decide, I support you. After what you're doing for me, I'd do anything for you." His eyes are damp for a moment before he blinks. "I gotta go. I'm almost drunk, and Anya will be irritated if I come home soused."

"Yeah." I nod. "Me too. Lara will wonder where I am."

"All right, man." He hugs me. "Let's do this again soon."

"Definitely." I hug him back. "Take care of yourself and Anya. I'll see you this weekend."

"See you then." He smiles at me, and we part ways. It's good to know he's always there, and I can always count on him.

Chapter 3—Jessica

I'M SLEEPING WHEN MY phone rings. It wakes me from REM, and a glance at the clock reveals it's two a.m. I've been home from the hospital for only three hours, and I groan when I see Embry's name on the caller ID. "No," I say in lieu of hello, "I'm too exhausted to fill in for someone."

"Oh, honey, it's not that." Embry sounds like she's about to cry. "I'm sorry to bother you, but I thought you should know. It's about Anya and Holt. They were in a car accident. You need to get here as fast as you can."

"What?" I sit bolt upright. "Are they okay?"

"I don't know, Jessica." Embry's voice breaks. "I just saw the ambulance come in when I was passing through ER, coming back from the cafeteria. I recognized her and Holt from that barbeque they hosted last summer and invited most of us."

"Thanks, Embry," I say, my mind racing. "I'll be right there." As soon as I hang up, I throw on clothes. My mind is racing, and I'm on the verge of tears. Anya is the only family I have besides her baby in my belly. She can't be seriously injured. It's unthinkable.

I drive to the hospital in a daze, barely remembering the trip. When I arrive, I park and rush inside, heading straight for the ER. I find Embry in the waiting room and give her a hug. She looks at me with tear-filled eyes. "I'm so sorry, Jessica. I wish I had better news for you."

I nod, afraid to ask. "How bad is it?"

Embry shakes her head. "It doesn't look good. They're doing everything they can, but it doesn't look like she's going to make it. Holt died on impact. She was trapped in the car for a long time. She lost a lot of blood. She's currently unconscious, but she's been in and out, asking for you. Go on in."

"Someone needs to call Maddox. He's going to be devastated. And Holt's parents." I feel numb as I say that before bracing myself to see Anya. It can't be the last time. It just can't.

"I think they're enroute," says Embry behind me.

I nod as I pass through the metal door and into the ER. The smell of antiseptic and blood is strong, but I can't focus on that. I rush to the bed where Anya lies, her face pale and her eyes closed.

My heart pounds, and my stomach churns as I reach for her hand. "Anya? Can you hear me?"

Her eyelids flutter, but she doesn't open them. Her lips part, and she whispers, "Holt."

I squeeze her hand and lean closer. "It's Jessica. Holt..." Should I tell her?

"Jessica."

I nod and stroke her hair back from her face. "Yes, I'm here. You're in the hospital."

"Charlotte," she croaks.

My heart clenches, and I lean forward to kiss her forehead. "I'm here, and she's fine. We're both fine."

Her eyes flutter open, and she looks around, seeming confused. "Where?"

"You're in the hospital, sweetheart. Do you remember what happened?"

She shakes her head and winces before suddenly sobbing. "Holt is dead."

I take her hand, ignoring the IV in it. "Yes, he is, but you're alive. You're safe."

She looks at me with surprising lucidity. "I'm dying. I can feel it, and you need to know about Maddox. He's Charlotte's father."

I want to believe she's confused, but her gaze is clear. I grasp her hand. "No, honey, I'm carrying yours and Holt's baby. Maddox has nothing to do with it."

"He donated sperm. We couldn't conceive, and we both wanted a child so badly. You're carrying my baby, but Maddox is Charlotte's biological father. You need to know because I want you to raise Charlotte together."

I can barely comprehend what she's saying, but I don't want to hear anymore. I don't want to waste any time I have left with her by arguing or being angry that she didn't tell me.

She's fading fast.

"I'm sorry," she whispers. "Please forgive me. Please remember to tell her about me. Tell her I loved her."

"I will," I promise, holding her hand tightly.

"I love you too, Jessica. Thank you for giving me a child. You're my best friend and sister, and I know you'll be the best mother she could ever have."

"I love you too, honey. We'll never forget you. Charlotte will always know how much her parents loved her, and how hard they fought to have her." The words are choked, and I squeeze her hand. "You can go now, sweetheart. It's okay. We'll be okay."

She nods, and her eyes flutter closed. Her hand goes limp, and I keenly feel the loss of her touch. I don't want to let go, but I force myself to rise. I kiss her forehead and whisper goodbye before walking out of the hospital room for the last time.

The nurse is waiting outside, and she gives me a sympathetic look. "I'm sorry for your loss, Ms. Malone." She nods to the waiting room. "Mr. Tillman is in the waiting room."

I nod and walk that way, steeling myself to face him. He's standing by Lara, but she's not holding him, to my surprise.

I'm compelled to cross the waiting room, and we move as one to hug each other. I can barely tolerate him, but he's the only one who understands how I feel right now.

"Is Anya...?"

"No. She didn't make it."

His arms tighten around me, and I cling to him for a moment. When he releases me, tears are streaming down my face. He brushes them away gently and then tucks me into his side.

"I'm sorry," he whispers. "I know you loved her like a sister."

"I'm sorry too," I tell him. "You lost your best friend."

"I didn't even get to say goodbye." He dissolves into sobs. I glanced at Lara, expecting her to step in, but she just hovers nearby, patting his shoulder. It's pretty awkward from his fiancée.

"It hurts like hell, doesn't it?"

"Yeah," he whispers, wiping his eyes.

"I'm sorry." I rub his back, wishing there was something more I could do.

"I never got to say goodbye to Anya either." He sniffles. "We should get out of here. I don't want to be in the same place where they died."

"Okay." I need to talk to him about what Anya said, though I assume her synapses were misfiring near the end. Maddox can't really be the father of the baby in my womb.

"There's a diner..." Lara trails off. "I have an early meeting, so if you two are okay...?" She trails off, already moving to the exit.

I barely notice her leaving but it's callous. I clear my throat, trying to stop crying long enough to speak. "Do you want to get out of here?"

"Yeah. There are things we should figure out."

"Like the funeral?"

"Among other things." He takes my arm and leads me out of the hospital.

We make our way to the parking lot, and he opens the passenger side door of his BMW for me. I climb in, and he shuts the door before rounding the vehicle to slide in the driver's seat.

He starts the engine and pulls out of the parking lot. "I'm sorry about Lara. She's usually more caring than this."

"It's fine. I understand. She's a busy woman, and I'm a stranger to her."

"Still, she could have stayed with me. It's not like she has to be anywhere else." His jaw tightens. "I'm not sure how I feel about her right now."

"I'm not sure how I feel about anyone. It's all too fresh, and I'm in shock."

He reaches over to take my hand. "Me too. I can't believe they're gone. It doesn't seem real."

"I know." I wipe away more tears. "I keep expecting her to text me or call me to complain about the latest episode of whatever show she's watching."

"I know. It's like a nightmare I can't wake up from." He sighs. "I'm sorry, Jessica. I know you were close to her, and I can't imagine how you must be feeling."

My heart aches as I think of Anya, and I blink back more tears. "I don't know what to do without her. She was my family. I have no one else."

"You have me." He squeezes my hand. "I know we haven't always gotten along, but I'm here for you, and I'll always be there for Charlotte."

"Thank you." I swallow hard, trying to hold back more tears.

"Of course. You're not alone, Jessica. You have me, and you have Charlotte."

"I know." I bite my lip, not sure how to bring up what Anya told me.

"I'm serious. I know you're not my biggest fan, but I hope that'll change over time."

"I appreciate that." I take a deep breath and decide to broach the subject. "Anya told me something right before she passed."

"What was it?" He glances at me, concerned.

"She said you're the biological father of the baby." I watch his reaction carefully.

He looks shocked for a moment, but then he nods. "I am. I'm sorry I didn't tell you. It wasn't my secret to share."

I stare at him, stunned. "Why did you agree to do it? Were you sleeping with her?"

"No! Of course not." He shakes his head. "Holt had a vasectomy when he was younger because one of his ex-girlfriends lied and said she was pregnant. He didn't want to take the chance of getting another girl pregnant, so he got one, but the reversal failed. He and Anya wanted to have a baby and asked me to donate sperm."

This is a lot to take in, and I try to process it. "So, you never slept with Anya?"

"Never." He shakes his head. "I would never betray Holt like that, and I would never cheat on Lara. I love her."

"Then why did you agree to do it?"

"Because they were my best friends, and I wanted to help them have a baby. They were desperate, and I couldn't say no. I knew Holt was sterile, so I agreed to donate sperm and be the funnest uncle ever."

"But you're engaged to Lara."

"I know, but it's not like I was going to be involved in the baby's life in a paternal way. I figured it would be okay since I wouldn't be raising the baby. I would just be there if the baby needed a kidney someday or something." He gives a shaky smile that dissolves to tears. "Holt was meant to be her dad. He was supposed to raise that baby and love her as his own. Now he's gone, and I'll never see him again. I can't believe he's not coming back."

I reach over to take his hand though I'm still in shock from this revelation following losing Anya and Holt. "I'm so sorry, Maddox. I know you loved him like a brother."

"He was my brother." He wipes his eyes. "I'm sorry for breaking down in front of you. I know you're hurting too, and I shouldn't put this on you."

"It's okay. I understand. I'm glad you're being honest with me, and I'm glad you're not the kind of guy who would sleep with his best friend's wife. I always thought you were an asshole, but maybe I was wrong."

He laughs. "I'm not perfect, but I'm not that bad. I would never do anything to hurt Holt or Anya. I would never do anything to hurt Lara or you."

"I guess I owe you an apology for judging you so harshly."

"It's okay. I get it. I'm a rich playboy, who gets everything he wants. I can't blame you for thinking the worst of me." He shrugs. "I'm not a saint, but I'm not a total douchebag either."

"I'm starting to see that." I offer a tentative smile. "We should probably talk about what happens next, but I don't think I can handle it right now. I just want to go home and cry until I fall asleep."

"That sounds like a good idea. Why don't I take you home, and we can talk tomorrow?"

"Okay. Thank you." I settle back in the seat, relieved that I can postpone facing reality for a few hours.

Maddox drives me home and walks me to the door. "I'll call you later, okay?"

"Okay." I unlock the door and turn to him. "Thanks for the ride home and everything else."

"Anytime. Goodnight, Jessica. Get some rest and take care of yourself and Charlotte. I'll check on you tomorrow." He kisses my forehead before turning to leave.

I watch him go, surprised by the tenderness in his actions. Maybe he's not the arrogant jerk I thought he was after all.

I lock the door behind him and head to the bedroom. I collapse onto the bed and start sobbing as the full weight of the day hits me. I can't believe Anya is gone, and I'm devastated by her loss. I also can't believe Maddox is the biological father of the baby growing inside me. It's a lot to take in, and I'm overwhelmed by it all. I cry myself to sleep, hoping that when I wake up, it will all have been a terrible dream.

Chapter 4—Maddox

AFTER I DROP OFF JESSICA, I'm emotionally drained as I drive home. Lara is in the shower when I get home, but it doesn't matter. I'm not inclined to turn to her for comfort right now.

Not that there's any comfort to be found. Nothing can make this better.

I strip down and climb into bed, closing my eyes. I'm exhausted, but I can't sleep. My mind is racing, and I can't stop thinking about Holt and Anya.

They were my best friends, and I can't believe they're gone. It seems unreal, like a nightmare from which I can't wake. I keep expecting to hear Holt's voice, laughing and teasing me about something stupid. I keep expecting to see Anya's smiling face, lighting up the room with her infectious joy, but it's not to be. They're gone, and I'm left alone in a world that suddenly feels cold and empty.

My heart breaks as I think of their little girl, Charlotte, who will never know them. She'll never know the love of her parents or the comfort of their embrace. She'll never hear their voices or feel the warmth of their presence. She'll grow up without them, and it crushes me to think of her missing out on such an important part of her life.

I'm determined to be there for her, to fill the void that Holt and Anya's absence will leave in her life. I never planned to be a father, but I can't ignore the biological connection now. I can't abandon her, and I won't. She's my flesh and blood, and I'll do whatever it takes to be a good father to her. I might never have wanted children, but I can't deny that I love her already.

I need to tell Lara, but I don't have the strength right now. Grief settles over me like a heavy blanket, suffocating and oppressive. I close my eyes but can't escape the pain.

I finally drift off to sleep, but it's restless and filled with nightmares. I wake up in a sweat, my heart pounding. It's early morning, and Lara is gone. I don't know where she is, and I don't care. I'm not in the mood to deal with anything, and I don't want to face the world.

I drag myself out of bed and stumble into the bathroom. I splash water on my face and brush my teeth, trying to shake off the lingering effects of the night. I'm numb, and everything feels surreal. It's like I'm stuck in a nightmare from which I can't awaken.

I dress and head downstairs, where I find Lara in the kitchen. She's dressed for work and sipping coffee at the counter.

"How are you doing?" she asks, looking up from her phone.

"I've been better." I pour myself a cup of coffee and sit across from her.

"I'm sorry, Maddox. I know you were close to them." She reaches out to touch my hand, but I pull away.

"Yeah. They were my best friends." I take a sip of coffee and try to gather my thoughts. "I needed you last night."

She bites her lip but says, "You had their other friend, and I don't deal well with emotional scenes."

"I know, but you could have tried. You could have been there for me."

"I'm sorry, Maddox. I'm not good at that sort of thing. You know that." Her tone is defensive.

"I know, but I needed you. I needed someone to comfort me, to hold me and tell me everything was going to be okay."

"I'm not good at that kind of stuff, but if you want a hug, I can give you one now." She stands and wraps her arms around me.

I stiffen, not wanting her comfort, but I allow it. It's the least she can do after abandoning me last night.

"I'm sorry, Maddox. I know you're hurting, and I wish I could make it better, but I'm not good at that sort of thing. I'm sorry."

"It's fine. I just need to be alone right now. I need to process everything." My tone is flat.

"I understand. I have to go to work, but if you need anything, please let me know. I'll be there for you, Maddox. I promise." She kisses my cheek and leaves.

I'm left alone with my thoughts, and I'm not sure if that's a good thing. Reluctantly, I call Holt's parents. Surely, they've heard, but they didn't come to the hospital.

His mom answers. "Hello, Hilary."

"Maddox, darling, how are you?" She sounds distracted.

"I'm...not good. I'm calling about Holt and Anya. Have you heard?"

"Yes, I heard. It's a tragedy. Holt was such a good boy. I can't believe he's gone." Her voice cracks.

"I'm sorry, Hilary. I know you're grieving, but I need to know what you and Andrew plan to do about the funeral arrangements."

"I told the home to do whatever they'd like. Andrew can't get away until the service, and I don't think I can deal with the arrangements."

I roll my eyes, irritated but not surprised by his parents' apathy. "I'll handle the arrangements then. Do you have a preference for the location?"

"I suppose the cemetery where his grandparents are buried is fine. We can pick out a plot for him there." She pauses. "I assume Anya's family will want to bury her with her parents."

I wince. Eight years, and she can't remember Anya is an orphan? "Hilary, Anya doesn't have any family. She was an orphan, remember?" She was left in a park at age four and never managed to track down her biological relations, so I don't even know if her parents are alive or dead. I just know Anya considered them dead to her.

"Oh, yes, that's right. I'm afraid there's no room at the family plot. Maybe pick a location where they can be interred together? I'm sure that would be what they would have wanted."

I sigh, exasperated. "Fine. I'll take care of it. What about the memorial service?"

"I'm sure the home has some ideas. They can contact me, or you can take care of it, dear. Whatever you think is best."

"I'll take care of it. Is there anything else I should know?"

"I don't think so. I'm sorry, Maddox, but I have to go. I have a luncheon with the ladies from the garden club. Take care, dear." She hangs up.

I stare at the phone in disbelief. How can she be so callous? I shake my head at the absurdity of it all. I should have known that Holt's parents would be useless. They never cared about him as much as they cared about appearances.

I sigh and pull out my laptop. I need to figure out what to do about the funeral and the memorial service. I have no idea where to begin, but I know I need to do something. I call Jessica and ask if she wants to help. She agrees, and we spend the day making plans. It's a somber task, but it helps to have someone with whom to share the burden.

We arrange for a joint funeral and memorial service to be held at the local church where Holt and Anya got married. It's a beautiful old building, and it seems fitting to celebrate their lives there.

I make the necessary calls to the home and the cemetery to make the arrangements. It's a lot of work, but it's a distraction from the grief that threatens to overwhelm me.

THE MORNING OF THE funeral is bright and warm, and I glare resentfully at the sun as I join Jessica on the steps of the church.

"It should be raining," I mutter. "It should be pouring down rain. That's what the weather should be like at funerals."

Jessica offers a sad smile. "Maybe it's their way of saying goodbye. Maybe it's the universe's way of telling us that they're in a better place now."

I snort. "I doubt it. The universe is a cruel and unforgiving place."

"Absolutely." She sounds as defeated as I feel. "Where's Lara?"

"Stuck in traffic after rushing off to babysit her client."

"I'm sorry. She should be here."

"She should be, but she's not." I shrug. "I'm used to it. She's always putting her career first."

She squeezes my bicep in a tender way. "I'm sorry, Maddox. I know today must be hard for you."

"It is, but I'm glad you're here. I don't think I could do this alone."

"Me neither." She clasps my hand. "Let's go inside. It's almost time."

We enter the church and take our seats in the front row. The pews are packed with friends and family, and I spot Holt's parents sitting in the front, their faces impassive.

I'm struck by the enormity of the moment and the finality of it all. I can't believe they're gone, and I'm overcome by a wave of grief. Tears well in my eyes, and I blink them back, trying to remain composed.

As the minister begins the service, I struggle to focus on his words. It's a beautiful sermon, but I can barely pay attention. My mind is a jumble of emotions, and I'm struggling to keep it together.

I glance at Jessica beside me and see tears streaming down her cheeks. I reach out and take her hand, offering what little comfort I can. She squeezes my hand and hands me a tissue as I lose the fight to suppress my tears.

We listen to the eulogies and sing hymns, and I try to absorb the solemn atmosphere. It's hard to believe this is real, that my best friends are gone forever.

When the service ends, we follow the coffins outside to the waiting hearses. The crowd of mourners is large, and I'm grateful for the support. It's a bittersweet moment, and I'm not sure how to feel.

We stand by the graveside as the coffins are lowered into the ground. It's a surreal experience, and I feel like I'm watching it happen to someone else. When the graveside service ends, Tanner Jensen approaches. He went to university with me and Holt before going to law school. He's a good guy, and I'm glad he's here.

"Hey, man." He pulls me into a hug. "I'm so sorry for your loss. Holt was a great guy."

"Thanks, Tanner. It means a lot that you're here."

"I'm here to mourn, but I also need to talk to you." He looks at Jessica. "You too."

"What's going on?" I ask, confused.

"I'm Holt's lawyer, and I need to discuss the terms of his will with you both."

"Now?" Jessica frowns.

"No, but soon. It's important."

"Okay." I nod. "We can meet later this week."

"Good. I'll set up a meeting. In the meantime, if you need anything, please don't hesitate to call me."

"I appreciate it, Tanner. Thanks for being here."

"Of course. Holt was a good friend, and I'm here to support you guys."

I watch as he walks away. I wonder what Holt's will contains and what it means for me and Jessica. It has to be about Charlotte.

After the funeral, we head back to Anya and Holt's home. There's a reception planned, and I'm not sure I'm ready to face it.

Jessica seems as reluctant as I am, but we steel ourselves and walk into the room. It's crowded with people offering condolences and sharing memories of Holt and Anya. It's a surreal experience, and I'm not sure how to react.

I'm grateful for Jessica's presence, and we stick close to each other as we navigate the sea of mourners. Lara arrives late, but she doesn't approach me. Instead, she goes straight to Holt's parents, offering her condolences. I'm not surprised, but it still stings.

She eventually makes her way to me and Jessica, offering a weak apology. "I'm sorry, Maddox. I tried to get here sooner, but I got caught up in work."

"It's fine. I'm used to it." I can't hide the bitterness in my tone.

"I'm here now. That's what matters." She tries to sound reassuring, but it falls flat.

"Sure. Let's get a drink." I lead her to the bar and order two glasses of wine.

As we sip our drinks, I notice Lara's gaze drifting toward Holt's parents. She's clearly more interested in maintaining her social status than comforting me, and it's a painful reminder of why our relationship isn't working.

I'm not sure how long I can continue to pretend otherwise.

The reception drags on, and I'm relieved when it finally comes to an end. I say goodbye to Jessica and head home. It's been a long and exhausting day, and I'm ready to collapse into bed and forget about everything.

Chapter 5—Jessica

I WATCH AS THE LAST of the mourners file out of the room, leaving me alone with my grief. I'm not sure how to feel. On the one hand, it's a relief to be alone with my thoughts, but on the other, I feel lost and adrift. Charlotte picks that moment to kick me. It's a light, fluttering sensation, and Anya died before she ever got a chance to feel it from the outside.

The thought crushes me, and I slump into a pew, sobbing until the owner of the funeral home comes to gently assist me out. He calls me a taxi since I couldn't have driven in my current emotional state.

I arrive home and collapse on the couch, unable to move. I'm exhausted and overwhelmed, and I'm not sure how to cope with my new reality. How can I go on without Anya? How can I raise a baby without her?

I'm not sure how much time passes, but I'm startled by a knock on the door. I drag myself off the couch and answer it, surprised to see Maddox standing there.

"Hey." His voice is soft. "I wanted to check on you."

"I'm okay." I'm not, but I don't want to admit it.

"Can I come in?"

"Sure." I step aside to let him in. "Sorry for the mess."

He waves a hand. "Sorry for coming by so late. I couldn't sleep. I had to get out of that house."

I nod, understanding his sentiment. "It's okay. I couldn't sleep either."

"Do you want to talk about it?" He sits on the couch.

"Not really. I just want to forget about everything for a while." I sit next to him.

"I know the feeling."

We sit in silence for a few moments, neither of us knowing what to say. The silence is broken by the baby kicking again, and I place a hand on my stomach.

"Is she moving?" he asks, sounding curious.

"Yeah. She's been pretty active tonight."

"May I?" He gestures to my belly.

"Sure." I take his hand and place it on my stomach. "There. Did you feel that?"

"I think so." A small smile appears on his face. "That's incredible."

"It is." I smile back, enjoying the moment before my smile fades. "Anya tried to feel her a few days ago, just after I noticed the first little kicks, but couldn't yet. It was the last time we spoke."

"I'm sorry, Jessica. I know this is hard for you." He looks down at his shoes. "I'm worried about you."

"I'm worried about me too." I laugh bitterly. "I have no idea what I'm doing, especially now that Anya and Holt aren't here to help me."

"I'm here for you and Charlotte. I want to help you through this."

I nod, touched by his offer. "Thank you." We fall silent again, and I lean my head against his shoulder. It feels natural, comfortable.

"Have you thought about what you're going to do now?" he asks after a few minutes.

"Not really. I guess I'll have wait to see what Mr. Jensen has to say. I'm going to call him in the morning to try to get it over with. Once I know the terms of the will, I can make a better plan. I'm hoping the estate can help me with the baby, even though it's not biologically mine. I don't know what I'll do if they refuse."

"I don't think they'd do that. Holt and Anya loved you like a sister, and I'm sure they considered what would happen to you and the baby in their will. If they didn't, I'll make sure you're taken care of, no matter what it takes."

I look up at him, moved by his words. I'm not used to anyone taking care of me, and it feels nice to have someone in my corner, even if he's doing it because Charlotte is his biological daughter. "Thank you, Maddox. I appreciate that."

"You're welcome. I meant what I said. I want to help."

"I know, and I'm thankful for that, but this whole thing is terrifying." My voice breaks. "How am I supposed to do this without Anya?"

"I don't know, but I'll help you. We'll figure it out together. I promise."

I nod, trying to believe him. "Okay. Thank you."

He puts an arm around my shoulders and pulls me close. I rest my head against his chest, and he strokes my hair. My eyes start to feel heavy, and I blink. "You should probably move me. I'm about to fall asleep." I haven't slept well since the accident, and it's all catching up with me.

"Nah," he says with confidence as he leans back, rearranging us so we're both more comfortable. "I'll stay a while if you don't mind. I don't want to be alone either."

I think about reminding him he has Lara, but after the way I've seen her act in the last few days, I'm not sure he does. "Okay. I don't mind. Just wake me if I start snoring or drooling."

"I will. Now, go to sleep. You and Charlotte both need it."

I close my eyes, and within seconds, his comforting scent and warmth lulls me to sleep. I wake up some hours later, disoriented and confused. It takes me a minute to realize I'm in my living room, and Maddox is still there, his arms wrapped around me.

He's fast asleep, and I take a moment to study his handsome features. He looks peaceful and relaxed, and I find myself smiling. He's been a rock for me these past few days despite his own grief, and I have to seriously reevaluate my opinion of him.

Careful not to wake him, I slowly extricate myself from his embrace and head to the bathroom. After using the toilet and washing my hands, I splash cold water on my face and stare at my reflection in the mirror. I look tired and worn down, but I also feel better than I have in days. I'm not sure what to make of that.

I head back into the living room and find Maddox awake and stretching.

"Hey," he says, rubbing his eyes. "What time is it?"

I glance at the clock. "About seven. Do you have to work?"

He shakes his head. "I took bereavement leave. Even my dad didn't give me a hard time about 'dropping the ball' for a change."

"Same, on the bereavement leave, that is." I pad to the kitchen. "I'm going to make breakfast. You can stay if you want, and then we can see if Mr. Jensen can get us in?"

"Sounds good. I'm starving."

I put on the kettle. "I hope tea is okay. I promised Anya I wouldn't drink coffee right now, so I haven't bothered to buy any."

"Tea's fine." He follows me into the kitchen. "Need any help?"

"No, I've got it. Make yourself at home."

I busy myself with making scrambled eggs and toast. It's a simple meal, but it's all I have the energy for right now.

Maddox helps me carry the plates to the table, and we eat in companionable silence. It's a far cry from the awkwardness of the first night we met eight years ago, when we took an instant dislike to each other.

Or maybe not. As I think about it now, I squirm. I immediately judged him to be a useless playboy billionaire, who'd inherited his parents' money, and I treated him accordingly. I'm not proud of it right now as I realize I fired the opening salvo in our years-long clash.

"What is it?" asks Maddox, pulling me from my thoughts.

"Nothing. I was just thinking about the night we met."

He chuckles. "Ah, yes. The infamous night that started it all. Holt was so pissed at me for being late and ruining his plans for a quiet dinner with you and Anya."

I smile, remembering how annoyed Holt was. "I was pretty mad at you too. I thought you were rude and arrogant."

Maddox grins. "I was. I was also drunk and hungover. Not a good combination. But I was also intrigued by the beautiful woman who was glaring daggers at me."

My cheeks heat at the compliment. "I wasn't exactly making a good impression either. I was judging you based on stereotypes and rumors I'd heard. I'm sorry for that."

"It's okay. I was a bit of a dick. I deserved it." He smiles sheepishly.

"A bit?" I tease.

"Okay, a lot, but I'm not that guy anymore. Or at least, I try not to be."

"I can see that. You've grown up a lot since then."

"So have you." He winks. "Seriously, you're not the same girl I met that night. You're stronger, more confident, and more determined. Still scathing about wealth though."

I can tell he's teasing by the way he winks but I respond seriously. "I've been as poor as someone can be, scrounging for my next meal out of a dumpster because my foster parents drank away the money they were supposed to use for my care. When I think about that and then imagine some of the frivolous ways people spend money...it upsets me. I'm aware it's a hangup. I know not everyone who has money is wasteful or selfish, but it's hard for me to separate the two sometimes."

"I understand. I grew up privileged, and I know I had it easy compared to most people. I also know that not everyone with money is a bad person, but it's hard to convince the world of that when so many of them are."

"Exactly. It's like no matter what you do, you can't escape the stereotype." I shake my head. "I'm sorry. I don't mean to rant."

"Don't apologize. I'm glad you feel like you can be honest with me. It's refreshing."

"I'm sorry. I know I'm not always the easiest person to be around." Managing a small smile, I add, "Especially hormonal and pregnant. I'm sure I'm a delight."

Maddox laughs. "I can handle it. I'm a big boy."

I blush, and my mind instantly goes to places it shouldn't. I quickly change the subject. "We should call Mr. Jensen and see if we can get in to see him today."

"Right. I'll call him now." Maddox pulls out his phone and dials the number. He speaks to the receptionist and arranges an appointment for nine-thirty. "Done. We have an hour to kill before we need to leave. What do you want to do?"

I take an exaggerated sniff of myself. "Take a shower. I smell like death warmed over." I wince as soon as the words are out of my mouth. "Sorry. Bad choice of words."

He gives me a sympathetic look. "It's okay. Go ahead and shower. I'll clean up the kitchen."

"Thanks. I won't be long."

I hurry to the bathroom, eager to wash away the lingering sadness from the previous day. I don't really stink, but I need some time to myself, and he's not going to follow me into the shower. Everything is upside down now, and I need to process it.

Maddox has been a godsend, but I'm not sure how to feel about the shift in our relationship. We've gone from barely tolerating each other to spending almost every waking moment together. It's a lot to deal with, and I'm not sure how to handle it. Yet I don't want him to go either. It's confusing and unsettling.

I push aside my conflicted feelings and focus on getting ready. I wash my hair and scrub my body until it's raw. I dress in a pair of black pants and a loose-fitting blouse. I don't want to look like I'm trying too hard, but I also want to appear professional.

When I emerge from the bathroom, Maddox is waiting for me in the living room. He offers me a cup of tea. "Here. This will help settle your nerves."

I accept the mug gratefully. "Thank you, though I'll regret it. It will just make me need to pee." Striving for a light tone to counteract the heaviness all around us, I say, "One of the joys of pregnancy. I can't even drink water without having to pee ten minutes later."

Maddox chuckles. "I can only imagine. I remember Holt complaining about Anya's constant trips to the bathroom. He always joked that she was drinking for two, but I never realized how literal that was." His expression fades. "Her miscarriages devastated both of them. I never got a chance to say it, but thank you for doing what you did for them." He looks at my stomach. "You were willing to sacrifice everything for their happiness. That's something special."

I shrug, uncomfortable with his praise as I struggle to keep my emotions in check. "It was nothing. I was happy to help. Anya was my best friend. She was like a sister to me. I would have done anything for her, and she would have done the same for me."

Maddox nods, and we lapse into silence. I finish my tea and set aside the empty mug. "We should probably get going. I don't want to be late for the meeting."

"Right. Let's go."

We drive to the lawyer's office in silence. I'm lost in my thoughts, and I assume Maddox is as well. Neither of us is looking forward to this meeting, but we need to know what Holt and Anya's wishes were for the baby.

Chapter 6—Jessica

WHEN WE ARRIVE, THE receptionist leads us to a conference room where Mr. Jensen is waiting for us. He greets us warmly and invites us to take a seat. He begins by expressing his condolences and then launches into the details of the will.

"Holt and Anya were proactive, modifying the wills when you hit thirteen weeks, Ms. Dawson."

"Jessica, please."

"Jessica. They made it clear that you and Maddox would share custody of Charlotte, but if the two of you couldn't reach an agreement, Maddox would have full custody. They also left a trust fund in Charlotte's name, which will be managed by a third-party custodian until she reaches the age of majority. The funds will be used for her education and care. If, for any reason, Maddox is unable to care for her, the funds will be transferred to you."

I nod, absorbing the information. "Does that mean I have to relinquish my parental rights?"

He gives me a kind smile. "You already did in the surrogacy agreement, but Anya and Holt wanted you two to raise her as co-parents. If neither of you want her, Holt's parents are the next option."

"I want her," I say passionately.

"His parents would make her miserable," says Maddox at the same time. A second later, he says, "I want her."

My heart stops for a beat. I never planned to raise the baby, but the last few days, I've started adjusting to the idea, and I want to. Now, he's going to take her from me.

"Jessica, look at me."

I blink, reluctantly looking at him. "She's your daughter, so it makes sense. I'm nothing to her." My voice breaks.

"That's not true." Maddox frowns at me. "She needs you. You're the one carrying her. You're the one who will feed and comfort her when she cries. She's going to bond with you more than she ever could with me."

"But you're her father."

"And you're her mother in every way that matters. You're the one who has carried her for months and who will be there for her in the years to come. I can't be a good father to her if I don't have you by my side."

I stare at him, shocked by his words. "You want to co-parent then?" He nods, and I remember how to breathe. "What about Lara? You should talk to her first. She might not like this arrangement."

"Lara will understand. She's not thrilled about the idea of kids, and she's not maternal. She doesn't even want kids with me, but she'll understand why I want to do this. She knows how close Holt and I were, and she knows I'll never forgive myself if I don't do this for him. For them. They were my family, and I owe them this much."

Mr. Jensen clears his throat. "If you're both in agreement, I can draw up the paperwork. It will be legally binding, and you'll both have equal rights and responsibilities as parents."

"Yes," I say before Maddox can change his mind. "I agree."

Maddox smiles at me. "Me too."

Mr. Jensen gets to work preparing the papers.

"Can I ask a question?"

He looks up at me. "Of course."

"How does this affect the surrogacy contract? Does that still stand?"

"It does, so you'll have to adopt her at birth, Jessica, but I'll prepare that and file the day she's born." He looks at Maddox. "Yours is clear cut. You're the donor, so you'll go on the birth certificate. Jessica will have to go through the adoption process. It's a little more complicated, but I'll make sure it's taken care of."

"Thank you, Mr. Jensen. I appreciate it."

"Call me Tanner. I'll be seeing a lot of you over the next few months."

I nod and turn to Maddox. "Do you have any questions?"

"Just one. When can we tell people about this? I don't want to lie to Lara, but I don't want to hurt her either."

Tanner answers, "The surrogacy contract is confidential, and the terms of the will are private, so there's no legal requirement to disclose the details of the arrangement. However, if you plan to co-parent, it might be best to be open and honest about it from the start. It will be a difficult adjustment for everyone involved, but it's better to be transparent."

"I agree." Maddox looks at me. "Are you okay with that?"

"Yes. I want to do what's best for Charlotte. I don't want her to grow up feeling like a secret or a burden. She deserves to know the truth and to have a loving family." I know all too well what it's like to be a burden to someone, and I won't have Anya's daughter ever feeling that if I can help it.

"She will. We'll make sure of it. Thank you for agreeing to this. I know it's a lot to ask, especially after everything you've been through."

"It's not a hardship. I love her already, and I want to do this. I just hope Lara is as understanding as you seem to think she is." My eyes widen. "Oh, no. Your parents. They're going to hate this. They're going to blame me."

Maddox takes my hand. "They won't. They might be surprised, but they'll understand. And if they don't, I'll make them understand. However they react, they can't blame you. I'm the one who agreed to donate the sperm. I knew the risks, and I accepted them. I'm not going to let anyone make you feel guilty about this. I promise."

I squeeze his hand, grateful for his support. "Thank you. I appreciate that. I know this isn't easy for you either."

"It's the right thing to do. I'm just sorry it has to be this way. Holt and Anya deserve to be here to see their daughter grow up, and she would have been theirs."

I nod my agreement. I never wanted to overstep, but now, I'm going to be Charlotte's mother. The thought is frightening but a little exciting. It's the only small bright spot I've seen in days.

We spend another hour with Tanner discussing the details of the will and the surrogacy contract. By the time we leave, my head is spinning, but I'm confident that we're doing the right thing.

As we walk to the car, I stop, placing a hand on my stomach. "Charlotte's kicking."

Maddox stares down at my belly. "Really? Can I feel it again?"

"Sure." I take his hand and place it on my abdomen. "There. Do you feel it?"

He nods, his eyes wide as he feels the baby move. "She's strong."

"She is." I smile. "I wonder if she knows what's going on?"

"Probably not, but she knows she's loved." Maddox looks at me with an intensity that makes me shiver. "We're going to be good parents to her, Jessica. We're going to give her the life they would have wanted for her."

"I know. We will because we love her and them."

Maddox wraps an arm around my shoulders. "Come on. Let's get you home. You need to rest, and I need to talk to Lara." He sounds like he's dreading it.

"When will you tell your parents?" I've heard stories about his parents and know they're just as socially conscious and obsessed with image as Holt's parents.

"When she's in college?" He smiles a bit. "Soon, but not yet. They're not overly interested in my life, so I doubt they'll care either way. Lara is the only one I really need to tell."

I hesitate. "We should talk to Holt's folks too. Andrew and Hilary probably don't know he's not the biological father. Maybe we should talk to them together and explain the situation."

"Maybe, but I'm not sure they'd care. They were never close to Holt, and they weren't exactly supportive of his marriage to Anya. They didn't approve of her, and they didn't approve of Anya and Holt using a surrogate. They're old-fashioned like that." His jaw clenches. "They have their own ideas about what's proper and acceptable. They wanted him to marry someone from their circle, and he refused. He loved Anya, and he wasn't going to give her up for anyone, so his father insinuated her inability to remain pregnant was meant to be."

"Because he didn't want her genes tainting his line?" I guess with a sick feeling in my stomach.

Looking disturbed, he shrugs. "He didn't say it just like that, but I heard him telling Anya to accept the truth that they weren't meant to procreate days after the second miscarriage."

"The one that went to eighteen weeks? God, what a horrible person. How could he say that to her?"

"I don't know, but it's the last straw. I'm not letting them anywhere near Charlotte. They don't deserve to be a part of her life and to poison her with their toxic views. We should tell them soon, but I think it will solve the problem by doing so—the trash will take itself out."

"Agreed." I sigh. "This is going to be a lot harder than I thought. I'm not sure I'm up to this. I had no idea how hard it would be to lose Anya and Holt, but I didn't realize how many people we'd have to deal with, and I'm not sure I'm equipped to deal with all the drama."

"I'll handle it. You focus on taking care of yourself and Charlotte. I'll manage the rest." He opens the passenger door. "Let's get you home. You need to eat and rest."

"I'm not hungry."

"Then you need to rest. Come on." He helps me into the car and closes the door.

I lean back against the seat and close my eyes on the ride home. I'm tired, but I can't sleep. I'm worried about what lies ahead. I'm also worried about Maddox. He's been amazing, but he's dealing with his own grief, and I'm afraid he's going to end up resenting all the changes in our lives—and he gets first choice of full custody if we can't make it work. The thought leaves a pit of dread in my stomach.

Chapter 7—Maddox

I DRIVE HER HOME, WALKING her up. She looks tired and fretful. I'd like to ease her mind, but I don't know how. I'm not sure there's a way to make this easier for her.

"I'll call you after I speak to Lara."

"Okay. Good luck."

"Thanks. I think I'll need it." I watch her walk inside and lock the door behind her.

When I get home, Lara is already gone for the day. She has a meeting with a new client, but she left a note saying she'll be home in time for dinner. I decide to use the time to clean up the apartment, but my mind keeps wandering to Jessica. She looked so sad and scared today. I wish I could do something to make her feel better. I hate that she's hurting.

After cleaning the kitchen, I sit down and call my parents. I plan to tell them, but when my mother answers, I just...don't. Mainly because she asks, "When are you coming back to work? Your father is trying to juggle everything himself."

I roll my eyes. She makes it sound like they're a struggling company, and I'm crucial when in reality, they have over a thousand employees just in the headquarters, where she and Father run things like the dictators they are. I don't even know why I'm still working there, other than it's expected.

"I'm not sure yet. I need some time to grieve." I try not to snap.

"Grieve? What is there to grieve? He was your friend, but you barely saw him these days. It's not like he was family."

I grit my teeth. "He was my best friend since childhood. Of course, I'm upset about his death. I can't believe you're not. Aren't you at least worried about how it looks if I don't take some time off to mourn him? The McEntires might judge you." My tone is full of sarcasm that I bet she doesn't detect.

"Well, yes, of course, I'm concerned, but we can't afford for you to take time off right now. We're in the middle of negotiations with three different companies, and we need you here to handle the contracts. Your father is swamped, and you know how important this is to him."

I bite my tongue to keep from screaming at her. "I don't think he's that busy. He can handle it. I need some time to myself right now. I'm sorry, Mother, but I'm not coming back to work. I'm taking bereavement leave. I'm sure Dad will find a way to cope without me."

"I'm not sure you understand how serious this is. If you don't come back to work, your father could fire you. He's in charge of the company, and he can do whatever he wants. You're lucky he hasn't fired you already. It's not like you're irreplaceable. There are plenty of qualified people who can do your job." Mother's voice is cold and unsympathetic. "You need to think about your future and what you want from life. If you want to stay employed, you need to get back here as soon as possible. Otherwise, you'll be out on the street with no money and no prospects."

I laugh bitterly. "I'm not worried about being unemployed, Mother. I have a trust fund that's more than enough to live on for the rest of my life. I don't need to work for you and Dad anymore. I'm done. I quit."

"Don't be ridiculous. You're not quitting. You're just going through a rough patch. I understand that, but you need to get over it and come back to work. Your father won't tolerate this behavior much longer. You need to get your act together and come back to work before it's too late. Act like a responsible adult."

I let out a grunt of frustration. "I'm thirty-one years old. I'm not a child, and I'm not coming back to work. I'm done. I'm finished with the company and with you and Dad. I can't do this anymore. I can't be who you want me to be. I'm not a puppet, and I'm not going to dance whenever you pull my strings. I'm done."

She sighs. "You're being dramatic, Maddox. You're acting like a spoiled brat, who's throwing a temper tantrum because he's not getting his way. Grow up. You're a grown man, and it's time you started acting like one."

"It's time I started living the life I want, not what you think I should have." I sound calm because I am. "I'll submit a formal resignation letter when I get around to it, but I quit. Goodbye, Mother."

"Don't hang up. We need to discuss this. I'm not sure you understand what you're doing. You're making a big mistake. You need to reconsider. Think about what you're giving up. This is your family. This is your legacy. You can't just throw it away because you're upset about something stupid. It's childish and immature. You need to grow up and stop acting like a child. I'm not going to stand by and let you ruin your life because you're being selfish and irresponsible. Do you really think Holt would approve?"

I suck air between my teeth to avoid cursing. "Yeah, I do, because he was about to tell his father to shove it and open his own restaurant after baby Charlotte is born. You know, before death robbed him of the chance to live his dream?"

She snorts. "That's a foolish decision. He was an intelligent young man, and he should have known better than to risk everything on a pipe dream. He had a good career and a bright future. He had everything going for him, and he was going to throw it all away for a silly fantasy. Maybe it's best for Andrew and Hilary that he passed before he could break their hearts like that. He was always a disappointment to them."

My hands curl into fists. "He was a human being, and he deserved to live his life however he chose. It's not up to you or me or anyone else to decide what's best for him. He made his own choices, and he was happy. But I'm not. I haven't been...ever. Not since I realized I was nothing more than a pawn in your game. I'm done. I'm out. Have a nice life, Mother."

"Maddox, wait!"

I hang up, shaking with rage. I want to scream and punch a wall. Instead, I grab a bottle of whiskey and pour myself a glass. I drink it straight, wincing at the burn. I need something to dull the pain. I don't know how to deal with this. I don't know how to make sense of the chaos swirling in my mind.

I drink until the room spins. Then, I stumble to the bathroom and puke. It's disgusting, and I feel like shit, but I don't care. I just want to forget. I want to erase the last few days from my memory and pretend none of this ever happened. I want to go back to when everything was normal and simple. Before Holt died. Before these confusing feelings for Jessica turned my life upside down.

I CRAWL INTO BED AND pass out. When I wake up, the sun is shining through the window, and my head is throbbing. I must have slept a ridiculous amount of time because it's early morning, and I remember it being midafternoon the last time I looked outside yesterday.

My head is banging, and the sound of the shower running sounds a thousand times louder than it should before it finally stops. Lara comes out in a towel and sits on the edge of the bed. "Hey, are you okay?"

"No." I groan, covering my face with my pillow.

"What's wrong?" She sounds genuinely concerned.

"Everything. I'm hungover, and I just had the worst conversation with my mother." My words are muffled by the pillow.

"Why? What happened?"

"I quit my job."

"You did what?" She sounds shocked.

"I quit. I'm done. I can't do it anymore. I can't be who they want me to be. I can't be their perfect son, and I can't be the perfect boyfriend. I can't be the perfect anything. I'm just...done."

She pats my arm. "Oh, Maddox, I'm so sorry. I know how hard this has been for you, but you can't quit your job. You love your job. You've worked so hard to get where you are. You can't just throw it all away because of a fight with your parents. They're your family. They love you, and they want what's best for you."

"No, they want what's best for them." I toss aside the pillow and sit up, wincing at the light. "I mean it, Lara. I'm not going back there. If that's a dealbreaker for you..." As I say it, I find myself hoping it is, and I know then this relationship is doomed.

She bites her lip before shaking her head. "Of course not. I want you to love your job as much as I love mine—speaking of, Felipe is in crisis mode again, so I have to go, but take some time off and figure out what you want to do next." She stands up, kissing my cheek before going into the closet to dress.

I lay back down, closing my eyes. I can hear her moving around the room, and then she's gone. I'm alone. Again. I didn't even think about telling her Jessica is carrying my baby. I don't know why. Maybe because I'm not sure she'd believe me. Or maybe because I don't want to hurt her. Either way, I feel like an asshole for not telling her sooner. I have to tell her. Tonight. After I sober up.

I drag myself out of bed and take a long, hot shower. The water feels good on my aching body, and I linger under the spray, trying to clear my head. When I finally emerge, I feel marginally better. I dry off and dress in jeans and a T-shirt. I'm not going back to work, and I don't want to wear a suit. I never want to wear a suit again.

I make coffee and toast, nibbling on the bread while I sip the dark roast. My phone beeps, and I see a text from Jessica.

Jessica: I have an ultrasound this morning if you want to come.
Maddox: I'll be there.

I finish my breakfast and head over to the hospital. When I arrive, Jessica is already in the exam room, and a nurse shows me where. I tap and wait for entry, finding her sharing the space with a woman in her mid-forties, who has close-cropped curls and lovely dark skin.

"This is Maddox," says Jessica to her. "Maddox, this is my midwife, Willow."

"Nice to meet you." I shake her hand.

"Likewise. Jessica's told me all about you. I'm so sorry for your loss. It's terrible. I knew Holt and Anya well. They were such wonderful people and never missed an appointment. I had the privilege of caring for Anya during her pregnancies, and I never met a woman who so badly wanted to be a mother." She seems genuinely on the verge of crying for a second. "Anyway, I'm glad you're here. Jessica needs support right now, and I can't imagine a better person to provide it than the father of her baby."

I nod, not sure what to say.

Jessica shyly smiles at me. "I'm glad you came."

"Me too." I smile back as I sit down in the chair beside her.

Willow clears her throat. "All right, let's get started. Are you ready to see your baby, Maddox?"

"Yes." I reach for her hand because it feels natural in the moment.

She squeezes my fingers, and I squeeze back as Willow squirts gel on Jessica's belly and presses the wand to her skin. The screen fills with a fuzzy image, and I stare at it, trying to make sense of what I'm seeing.

"There's the baby's heartbeat." Willow points to a small, fast-beating circle. "And there's the fetus. Looks like everything is developing normally."

My breath catches in my throat as I watch the tiny baby on the screen. It's so small and fragile, but it's alive, and it's growing. Tears prick my eyes, and I blink them away. I'm not sure why I'm so emotional, but I can't help it. Seeing the baby makes it real in a way that it wasn't before.

"Would you like to know the gender?" asks Willow.

"Yes," says Jessica eagerly.

"It's a girl."

A girl. A daughter. A little girl who will be half me and half Anya but raised by Jessica. Our little girl will be loved and cared for and cherished. A little girl who will change our lives forever. I smile down at her. "Anya was right."

Jessica nods, tears streaming down her cheeks. "She always insisted she'd be a girl, and she called her Charlotte from the time I got a positive pregnancy test."

I wipe away her tears with my thumb. "Thank you for doing this. For keeping her safe and healthy. I know it's not easy, and I appreciate it more than I can say."

"You're welcome." She sniffles.

We listen to the baby's heartbeat and see her move on the monitor, and then Willow prints photos for us. She wipes the gel off Jessica's belly, and we both stare at the pictures in awe. I hold the one of the baby's profile and trace her tiny nose and chin. She's perfect, and I can't believe she's growing inside Jessica.

"Do you mind if I keep this one?" I ask.

"Not at all." She smiles. "I have plenty. I'm going to frame one and put it on my nightstand, so I can see it every day."

"I'll do the same." Once I tell Lara. That makes my stomach lurch. I have to tell her. I can't keep this secret any longer. It's not fair to her, and it's not fair to the baby. It's time to come clean.

Jessica and I walk out of the room together and part ways in the hallway. I head home and stare at the profile pic off and on all day. I don't bother looking for a job. I just play the piano to fill the time until Lara comes home.

Except she texts me around dinnertime.

Lara: It'll be hours yet. Don't wait up for me.

Maddox: Okay.

I sigh and order pizza. I eat it in front of the TV, watching a basketball game. I can't concentrate and end up falling asleep on the couch. When I wake up, the apartment is quiet, and the clock says one a.m. I stretch and yawn, rubbing the sleep from my eyes.

I go into the bedroom and find Lara sleeping. She's curled up on her side, her dark hair spilling across the pillow. She looks peaceful and beautiful, and I hate to disturb her. I strip down to my boxers and climb into bed, careful not to wake her.

I lie awake for a long time, staring at the ceiling and wondering how the hell I'm going to tell her about the baby. I know she's going to be angry and hurt, and I don't blame her. I'm not sure how she's going to react, but it's not going to be good.

I finally fall asleep, but I don't rest well. I keep having nightmares about Lara leaving me and taking the baby with her. I wake up in a cold sweat, my heart pounding. I glance over at Lara, but she's still sleeping, and I know the nightmare has zero chance of ever coming true, because she's not going to want any baby, let alone try to steal mine.

My heart stops racing, and I wonder what woke me—until I realize my phone is ringing. I miss the call and realize I've missed two others from Jessica. It's not even five a.m., so my stomach knots with dread when I call back. "Jessica, what's wrong?"

"I'm bleeding." Her voice is choked with fear.

"How bad?"

"A lot."

"I'm coming to get you. Pack a bag. I'll be there in ten minutes."

"I'm already at the hospital. I just...don't want to be alone." She hangs up.

I jump out of bed and start dressing, waking Lara.

"What's wrong?" she mumbles.

"Jessica's bleeding. I have to meet her at the hospital."

"Bleeding? Is it the baby?"

"I don't know."

She sighs. "That's too bad, but why did she call you?"

"Because I'm the father, and she has no one else."

Lara sits up, blinking in the darkness. "What?"

"I'm the father of the baby. I was going to tell you, but I didn't know how, and I was afraid of how you'd react, and I'm sorry, but I have to go. She's waiting for me, and I have to make sure she and the baby are okay."

"Wait, Maddox, stop. What are you talking about?"

"I'll explain later." I hurry out of the room, grabbing my wallet and keys. Lara calls after me, but I keep going. I need to reach Jessica as soon as possible.

Chapter 8—Jessica

LYING HERE ALONE IN a bed on the OB floor is torture. I work these halls, but I'm not used to being the patient. Embry bustles in, smiling at me, but I can't force a smile in return.

"Willow is on her way," she says with a hint of forced cheer. "You know bleeding is common in pregnancies. It doesn't mean there's a problem with Anya's baby."

"It doesn't mean there isn't." I sound so pessimistic, but it feels like losing Charlotte is inevitable. I've already lost everyone else I care about, so why not her too?

"I'm here," says Maddox, bursting into the room. He obviously dressed quickly and is wearing mismatched running shoes. In spite of everything, I notice that, and it's endearing.

"Hi. Thanks for coming." I sound weak and pathetic.

"Of course." He comes to my side and takes my hand.

"Willow is on her way, and we'll run some tests to make sure everything is okay." Embry pats my arm. "Try to relax, Jessica. Everything will be fine."

I nod, but I don't believe her.

She leaves, and Maddox pulls a chair close to the bed. He holds my hand, his grip warm and reassuring. "I'm sure everything will be fine."

"Easy for you to say. You're not the one who might lose the baby."

He looks stricken. "I'd be devastated if anything happened to her. I know it's not the same, but I'm worried about her too. I'm worried about you."

Tears spring to my eyes. "I'm sorry. I shouldn't have said that. I just...I don't know how to handle this. I'm scared, Maddox, and I don't know what to do. I'm sorry I bothered you with it, but I didn't have anyone else…"

"Stop apologizing. I'm glad you called me. I want to be here for you and Charlotte." He squeezes my hand tighter. "I'm not going anywhere. We're in this together, okay?"

I nod, swallowing the lump in my throat. "Okay."

Willow comes in, and she looks tired. She's been working a double shift, and I feel guilty for calling her in. "Sorry to get you out of bed."

"Don't worry about it. Let's take a look at things, shall we?" She lifts the sheet and examines me. It's uncomfortable but brief. She frowns, and I have a sinking feeling in my stomach.

"What is it?" I ask.

"Your cervix is closed, but I'd like to do an ultrasound to check on the baby. I'll be right back." She hurries out of the room.

"What does that mean?" asks Maddox.

"The cervix is what controls whether or not the baby can be born. It's supposed to stay closed throughout the pregnancy, but sometimes, it opens prematurely. If that happens, the baby can't survive outside the womb. It's too early." I sigh. "An incompetent cervix is why Anya couldn't carry to term, and she never made it far enough along for a cerclage with two of them, and the cerclage didn't work with their son who was born at eighteen weeks."

He pales, maybe remembering like I am the pain of attending that memorial service and seeing the tiny coffin. "But yours is closed, right?"

"Right now, yes, but that could change." I try to remain calm, but I'm terrified. I can't lose Charlotte. I just can't.

Willow returns with the portable ultrasound machine and spreads gel on my belly. She moves the wand around, and the image appears on the screen. I hold my breath, searching for the baby's heartbeat. When I hear it, I let out a relieved sigh.

"Heartbeat looks good," says Willow with a smile. "Let's check the placenta. Hmm."

"Hmm, what?" I ask, my anxiety rising.

"It's low-lying, but that's not uncommon in a first pregnancy. It's likely it will move up, but in the meantime, you know what I'm going to say..."

I groan. "Bed rest."

"For at least a few weeks. I'm sorry, but it's important to give the placenta time to move up and prevent a preterm delivery. I know that's not what you want to hear, but it's what's best for the baby." She wipes the gel from my belly.

"I understand." I sigh.

"I'll get the paperwork started, and you can go home in a couple of hours. In the meantime, try to get some rest." She pats my shoulder and turns to Maddox. "Jessica is a busy beaver, so you're going to have your hands full keeping her in bed."

"It's not his problem," I say.

"I'll keep her in line," he says at the same time with smooth confidence and a wink at me.

I glare at him. "I'll take care of myself, thanks."

Willow gives me a scolding look. "How? Bed rest means only up and down for the bathroom. No cooking, no cleaning...no anything until you're off bed and pelvic rest. If you don't have a care plan in place, I can't discharge you."

"I can leave AMA."

She nods, looking unimpressed. "You could, but you won't."

"What's AMA?" asks Maddox, looking at Willow.

"Against medical advice," I answer for her, annoyed. "If I refuse treatment, they can't keep me here against my will."

"You wouldn't," he says, horrified.

"I would." I cross my arms over my chest. "I'm a nurse. I know what I'm doing."

"You're also pregnant and should be resting, not working." Willow shakes her head. "Don't be so stubborn and take some help." She snaps her fingers. "Won't the trust for Charlotte pay for a full-time nurse for you?"

I shrug. "Maybe. I'll ask Tanner."

"I'll ask him after we get you settled at my place." Maddox looks implacable, and Willow decides to scoot.

"I'll get the paperwork started." She hurries out of the room.

"Maddox, I can't let you do that. It's too much to ask of you and your girlfriend." I'm starting to panic.

"Lara won't mind."

"I'm so sorry. I didn't mean to cause problems between you and your girlfriend. I was just so scared, and I didn't know who to call. This isn't your probl—"

He presses two fingers against my lip, sending a spark through me at the light touch. "Shh. It's not a problem. Charlotte needs care, and I'll care for you to provide it. There's no need to entrust yourself to a stranger when you can stay with your hated foe." His smile is fleeting, but his voice is tender.

"I don't, you know? Hate you, I mean. I was just being a bitch." My cheeks heat, and I avoid his gaze.

"We were both being assholes, and that's in the past. Now, we're co-parents, and we have to work together to make sure Charlotte is safe and healthy." He sits on the edge of the bed and takes my hand again. "I promise to do everything in my power to keep you and the baby safe. Will you let me do that?"

I hesitate, but he seems sincere, and I can't deny the relief that floods through me. I have no one else, and he's offering to help. "I guess I don't have a choice."

"There's always a choice, but I hope you choose to let me help you. It would be my pleasure." He strokes the back of my hand with his thumb, and I shiver.

"Fine, but I'm paying you back. I don't want to owe you anything."

"You don't owe me anything. I'm the father of the baby you're carrying, and I'm happy to help. I want to help." A shadow crosses his face, and he looks away for a moment. When he looks back at me, he seems sad. "I want to be involved in Charlotte's life as much as possible. I want to be there for her and for you. I know this isn't what you planned, but it's what we have, and I'm willing to do whatever it takes to make it work."

His words surprise me, and I find myself nodding before I can think about it. Without thinking about it, I sway toward him. Realizing I'm about to lean in to kiss him, I immediately overcorrect and fall back against the pillow. "Sorry. I'm a little dizzy."

The way he responds with urgency makes me feel guilty for the white lie, but there's no way I'm admitting I almost kissed him. He's unofficially engaged, and we were enemies forever. It had to be...a moment of emotional vulnerability coupled with acute stupidity.

"Are you okay? Should I get a nurse?" he asks, his voice laced with concern.

"No, I'm fine. Just a little dizzy. It's probably from the blood loss. I'll be fine once I get some fluids." I look at the IV bag. "That should finish infusing in about forty minutes. Then I can go home."

"Good. I'll go talk to Willow and get the ball rolling." He stands and hesitates before leaning down to press a soft kiss to my forehead, and I try to hide my involuntary reaction. My skin tingles, and I stifle a shiver. What's wrong with me?

After he's gone, I stare after him, touching the spot where his lips brushed my skin. I'm confused and overwhelmed and don't know what to think. All I know is that I'm going to be staying with Maddox for the foreseeable future, and that scares the hell out of me. What if I fall for him? What if I fall for him, and he doesn't fall for me? What if he does?

My head spins with all the possibilities, and I close my eyes, trying to calm my racing heart. I can't let myself fall for Maddox Tillman. I can't. It would be the biggest mistake of my life, and I've made enough mistakes to last a lifetime. This is about Charlotte, not me. I need to remember that.

I take a deep breath and let it out slowly, trying to clear my mind. I focus on the steady beeping of the monitor, letting the sound soothe me. I have to stay calm and focused. I have to do what's best for the baby, even if that means spending time with Maddox, who I used to despise.

I can't believe I'm about to move in with the man I once thought was my nemesis, and I almost kissed him. I shake my head, trying to banish the memory from my mind. I'm almost successful when I think about Lara and groan aloud.

"Are you okay?" He comes rushing back in at the sound. "Do you need something?"

"I'm fine. I was just thinking about your girlfriend, and how she's going to hate me living with you." Partial honesty is better than a total lie, I guess.

His expression is inscrutable. "She'll understand. Lara is a reasonable person."

"I doubt that very much, but if you say so." I try to sound indifferent, but I'm not. I'm nervous about being in the same house as Lara while I'm attracted to her boyfriend. It's a recipe for disaster, and I don't know how to fix it.

"She will. Don't worry about it. I'll take care of everything." He pats my arm, and I try not to flinch. Every time he touches me, I feel a jolt of electricity, and it's unnerving.

"I can take care of myself. I don't need you to rescue me." I know I sound defensive, but I can't help it. I'm used to being independent and taking care of myself. I don't like feeling helpless and dependent on someone else.

"I know you can, but you don't have to. Let me help you. It's what friends do." His smile is disarming, and I find myself returning it, despite my reservations.

"We're friends now?" I raise an eyebrow at him.

He shrugs. "Why not? We're going to be raising a child together. That makes us family, and that makes us friends."

"I suppose it does." I can't argue with his logic, even though it feels strange to be friendly with the man I once loathed.

"So, friends?" He holds out his hand, and I reluctantly shake it.

"Friends." The word feels foreign on my tongue, but I know it's the right decision. I need Maddox's support, and I can't afford to alienate him. If we can't make it work, he gets custody. I need to be nice to him to keep Charlotte. Even as I think it, I know that's not the full reason, but I shove that to the back of my mind. I don't want to think about the complications tonight.

"Willow said she'll release you in an hour. I'll go get your prescriptions filled and pick up some groceries. Do you have any special requests?" He leans against the wall, looking casual and relaxed.

"I'm sure you have food at your house, and I'm sure it's more than adequate. You don't have to buy anything special for me."

He chuckles. "I'm sure it is, but you're pregnant and on bed rest. You need to eat healthily, and I have no idea what that means. I'll get a nutritionist to come by and help me figure it out, but I might as well spoil you a bit before she tells us what we can't eat right now."

I frown. "We?"

"Yes, we. I'm going to be eating the same stuff you are in solidarity, so it's easier if I just get everything for both of us." He grins. "Besides, I like to eat, and I'm not a fan of rabbit food."

I laugh despite myself. "I'm not either, but I'm also not a fan of hospital food. I'm sure whatever you get will be fine."

He nods. "I'll get a variety of things, and we can see what you like. I assume you don't have a preference for brands or anything like that?"

"Nope. I'm easy. Whatever you get will be fine. I'm not picky." Growing up hungry in various foster and group homes, I learned to eat whatever and whenever I could. It was the same for Anya. I swear half the reason she fell in love with Holt, at least in the beginning, was because he made such amazing food. That makes me sniffle.

He freezes. "What's wrong?"

"Nothing. I'm fine." I wave him off, but he doesn't seem convinced.

"You're not fine. You're crying. Are you in pain?" He looks alarmed.

"No, I'm not in pain. I was just thinking about Anya and Holt, and how she loved his cooking. He was a great cook, and I was just remembering..." I trail off as tears fill my eyes.

Maddox comes to my side and takes my hand. "Did they tell you he was going to open a restaurant after Charlotte's birth?"

I nod. "Yeah, he was so excited. He had a meeting with a chef to discuss the menu. He wanted to serve comfort food with a twist." I bite my lip. "Anya had complete faith, but I was afraid he might give into his parents' pressure and not live his dream after all once he got around to telling them."

"Holt yielded to them in the past, but he spoke with such passion that I'm sure he was going to make this happen. He was a good friend, and I know he would have been a great father." Maddox's voice is thick with emotion, and I squeeze his hand in sympathy.

"I'm sure he would have."

He looks frightened. "I don't know if I will. What do I know about being a father? Mine has always been too busy for me, and I never had a good male role model growing up. I have no idea how to do this."

His admission startles me, and I look up at him in surprise. "I'm sure you'll be a great father. You're already stepping up and taking responsibility for Charlotte. That's more than some men would do. That counts for a lot."

"I don't know. I'm scared, Jessica. I'm really scared. What if I mess it up?" He looks at me with wide eyes, and I realize he's as lost as I am.

"You won't. We'll learn together. We'll figure it out, and we'll be great." I'm not sure who I'm trying to convince more, him or me, but I feel a surge of optimism. Maybe we can do this. Maybe we can be a family for Charlotte.

"We will." He smiles, and I return it. Suddenly, I'm looking forward to living with him. It might not be so bad after all.

"I'm glad we talked. I'm glad we're on the same page." I yawn, suddenly exhausted.

"Me too. Get some rest, and I'll be back before you know it." He kisses my forehead again, and this time, I don't pull away. Instead, I lean into it, enjoying the warmth of his lips against my skin. It's a comforting gesture, and I need that right now. Just comfort. There's nothing more to it than that.

Chapter 9—Maddox

INSTEAD OF GOING TO the store, I place an order with the app to pick up in an hour at one of the twenty-four-hour grocers in the area. Bracing myself, I drive back to my apartment to face Lara before bringing home Jessica.

She's standing in the foyer when I step inside, and she looks pissed. "You're back. Good. Now explain to me how the hell you're the father of your best friend's wife's baby, who is currently growing in her best friend?" Her eyes narrow. "Did you cheat with her? Or with Jessica? Were you going to pass off your cheat baby as theirs?"

I roll my eyes. During my absence, she's clearly created some wild theories in her mind. "It wasn't like that. Holt and Anya were having trouble conceiving, and they asked me to help. I agreed, and they did IVF with my sperm. Jessica is the surrogate."

"Why the hell would you agree to that? It's so weird. And why didn't you tell me?" She crosses her arms over her chest, glaring at me.

"Because it was none of your business. It was between me, Holt, and Anya. I helped them because they were my friends, and I was trying to do the right thing." I sigh. "I was never meant to be the father, Lar. I was going to be Uncle Maddox, and I was totally fine with that. You don't want kids, and I didn't either, so I...don't know. Maybe it was a bit of a selfish way to pass on my DNA, but it seemed harmless. In fact, it was positive, because it helped the man who was like a brother to me. I thought I was doing the right thing."

"You still should have told me. I had a right to know." She frowns. "Now you have a baby coming, and I don't want one."

"You don't have to be involved. I'll take full responsibility. I'll hire a nanny and everything." I run a hand through my hair. "Look, I'm sorry.

I fucked up. I thought it was the right thing to do at the time, and I didn't think it would come to this." I don't tell her I have no regrets about the decision—just how it turned out, making me and Jessica parents instead of Anya and Holt.

"I don't like your seed germinating in some other woman's body. You had to know I'd hate the idea." She pouts.

"I didn't think you'd care, because you never wanted children." I shake my head. "This is a terrible time for this conversation. I have to go pick up the groceries and bring Jessica here. She's on bedrest."

Lara glares at me. "What do you mean, you have to go pick her up? Why is she coming here?"

"Because she needs to be on bedrest, and I'm not leaving her alone. She doesn't have anyone else, and she's my responsibility. She's carrying my child, and I'm not abandoning her." I hold my ground, refusing to back down.

"Your child? It's hers. She's the surrogate. You're not the father. You're just the donor. That's what you said." She raises an eyebrow.

"I changed my mind after the accident. I want to be a part of the baby's life. I want to be involved in the pregnancy. I owe that to Holt and Anya." I take a deep breath. "I'm sorry, Lara. I know this isn't what you wanted, but it's what I need to do. I hope you can respect that."

She stares at me for a long moment, and I can see the wheels turning in her mind. Finally, she sighs. "Fine. I'll pack my things. I'm moving out."

"You don't have to. I told you, I'll hire a nanny. I don't expect you to be involved." I reach for her, but she pulls away.

"No. I can't stay here. Not with her. Not with the baby. It's too much. I'm sorry, Maddox, but it is." She bites her lip. "I need to tell you something anyway..."

"What?" I sound impassive and realize I don't feel much of anything right now.

Lara wrings her hands. "It was just a kiss... I didn't mean for it to happen, but he makes me feel things you don't and never have." She looks troubled and near tears.

I'm stunned, but I can't pretend I haven't thought about kissing Jessica, so I can't feel too betrayed that she kissed someone else. "Who?"

She blinks. "Felipe. Felipe Morney. He's been flirting with me for months. I thought it was harmless, but then he kissed me, and I felt something. Something I've never felt with you. He's a rockstar, Maddox. My parents will disown me. I wanted to make the safe choice, so I told him no..."

I pat her arm, feeling surprisingly fine with this turn of events. "I don't ever want to be anyone's safe choice. We both deserve better than that. Go chase your dreams, Lara. If he's what you want, go for it. I wish you luck."

Her mouth drops open, and she gapes at me. "Are you serious?"

"I am. I'm not in love with you, Lara." I rake my hand through my hair. "I've been struggling to admit that to myself and then to you for a while. I'll always love you, but you're like my sister more than a lover. I'm not in love with you, and I don't think you're in love with me. This is for the best."

Tears fill her eyes, but she nods. "I'm not. I'm not in love with you. I thought I was, but I'm not. I'm in love with him. I don't know how to make it work with him, but I want to try." She throws her arms around me. "Thank you for understanding. Thank you for being so wonderful about it."

I hug her back. "I'm not wonderful. I'm relieved. I'm happy for you. I'm happy for both of us. I think we both needed this wake-up call."

"I think you're right." She steps back and wipes her eyes. "I'll go pack my things. I'm going to crash with a friend until I find a new place. I'll be out of your hair by the time you get back." Her expression turns worried. "Will you be okay? I'm worried about you and Jessica. You barely know her, and she's a stranger. She could be a gold-digger. She could be a crazy person. I don't want you to get hurt."

"She's not. She's a good person, and she's been through a lot. I trust her, and I know she wouldn't do anything to hurt me or the baby." I smile at her. "I appreciate your concern, but I promise I'll be fine. I have to go. I have to pick up the groceries and Jessica. She's waiting for me."

"Okay. I'll be gone by the time you get back." She hesitates long enough to squeeze my hand. "I hope your baby is okay. I want the best for you, Maddox, even if I'm not the one who gives it to you. You deserve happiness, so don't forget to keep yourself open to that. It may come from an unexpected source—like a rock star." She winces and giggles as she says that. "My dad is going to lose his mind."

"Good luck with that. I hope he comes around." I give her another quick hug before heading back to the car. I can't believe our relationship ended so easily, but I'm relieved. I'm also excited about the future.

As I drive to the grocery store, I think about Jessica and wonder if she'll be open to a relationship. I'm not sure if she's interested in me romantically, but I'm definitely attracted to her. I can't deny that. I'm also attracted to her personality and the way she cares so much about others.

Without Lara to act as a buffer and keep me from making a move, I'm worried I won't be able to hide my growing feelings. I should probably try to rein them in, but I don't want to. I want to explore them and see where they lead. I just don't want to frighten her or ruin our attempts at co-parenting.

When I arrive back at the hospital, Jessica is dressed and waiting for me. She smiles when she sees me, and my heart skips a beat. She's so beautiful, and I can't believe I was able to pretend I didn't notice that for so long.

"Hi. How are you feeling?" I ask as a nurse brings her discharge papers.

"Better. Ready to get out of here." She signs the papers and stands up from the bed to move to the wheelchair. "Thanks for picking me up."

"Of course. Let's get you home." I take her bag and walk with her to the car as the nurse pushes her in a wheelchair. "I assume you need to stop by your place and get some things?"

She hesitates. "I do, but I'm also supposed to get to bed as quickly as possible."

"Don't worry. I'll have someone get your stuff after you make a list. So, to my house..." I hoist her bag into the trunk as the nurse helps her into the passenger seat.

"To your house." She sounds resigned but not unhappy.

"I picked up some groceries, and I'll have a nutritionist come by tomorrow to help plan meals that are healthy and nutritious for the baby." I pull out of the parking lot and head toward my apartment.

"That's great. I'm sure she'll have lots of ideas." Jessica shifts in her seat. "Promise me that if Lara says no to this, you won't make a fuss or risk your relationship just to help me. I can hire a nurse."

"She's not saying no. She's moving out."

Jessica gasps. "Oh, Maddox. I'm so sorry. I didn't mean to break you guys up. I swear, I can find somewhere else to go. I don't want to cause problems for you."

"You're not. It was a mutual decision. She has a new boyfriend, and he's a rock star. She wants to pursue that and see where it goes. It's for the best. I'm not in love with her, and she's not in love with me." I hesitate. "I guess neither of us were in the right place to admit it until tonight. Our relationship has been strained for a while, but we both kept clinging to it out of familiarity and tradition. We both knew it wasn't working, but we were too afraid to say it."

"Wow. That must have been hard. Are you okay?" She puts her hand on my arm, and a jolt of electricity shoots through me.

"I'm fine. Relieved, actually. It's been brewing for months, and I think we both knew it was coming. Neither of us wanted to be the one to end it. I'm glad we finally did."

"I'm sorry it happened like this. I feel like I caused it." She bites her lip.

"You didn't. I promise. It's not your fault. It's mine and Lara's. We weren't in love, and we shouldn't have stayed together as long as we did. We were comfortable, and our parents approved of the match. They used to joke about us getting married as far back as I can remember." I shrug. "It was easy, and it was expected. Neither of us were brave enough to do what we really wanted, so we settled for what was convenient."

"I can understand that, but it sucks. I'm sorry you're hurting." She squeezes my arm.

"I'm not. I'm not in love with her, and I'm not sad. I'm relieved. I'm excited to move on and create a life with you and the baby." I realize how revealing that statement is and hold my breath. Fortunately, she doesn't seem to read too much into me including her in my new life.

"I'm excited too. I'm looking forward to getting to know you and raising Charlotte together. I'm sure she'll be lucky to have you as her father." She smiles at me, and my heart melts.

"I'm sure she'll be lucky to have you as her mother." I take her hand and squeeze it, resisting the urge to lift it to my lips and kiss it.

The rest of the ride passes in a companionable silence as we listen to music. When we arrive at the apartment, I carry her bags upstairs and show her to the guest room, which is next to mine. As promised, Lara is already gone, though a note on the kitchen table tells me she took the cat.

"Do you have any pets?" I ask, realizing I don't know if Jessica has allergies.

"No. I work a lot of hours, so it wouldn't be fair to have a pet. I've always wanted to adopt a dog, but I don't have the time. Maybe when Charlotte is older." She sits on the edge of the bed and yawns.

"Get settled. I'll get early breakfast started. The doctor said you could eat whatever you wanted as long as it was healthy, so I got a few things." I gesture toward the kitchen.

"Sounds good. I'm starving. I'll take a shower and join you in a bit. Thanks for everything." She smiles at me, and I feel warm all over.

"You're welcome. I'm happy to help." I leave her to settle in and head to the kitchen to cook breakfast. I decide to make omelets with spinach, mushrooms, tomatoes, and cheese. They're simple but filling and should be healthy for the baby and Jessica.

While they cook, I set the table and brew some coffee before remembering she can't drink that now. Lara has a kettle, and it's still under the cabinet when I search for it, so I start some hot water too. As the eggs cook, I hear the shower turn off and the bathroom door open. A few minutes later, Jessica emerges wearing a pair of yoga pants and a T-shirt. Her wet hair is pulled back into a ponytail, and her face is scrubbed clean.

The T-shirt stretches gently over her burgeoning belly, revealing about an inch of her creamy brown skin above her pants, and the sight is mesmerizing.

"Something smells delicious." She walks over to the stove and peers at the pan. "Omelets? I love those but rarely have the time to make them."

"They're almost done. Have a seat." I motion to the table. "I made you tea. I hope you like chamomile."

"I do. That's perfect. Thank you." She sits down and pours herself a cup. "How are you doing? Feeling okay with everything?"

"Yeah. I'm good. I'm glad to have you here." I dish up the omelets and bring them to the table.

She tilts her head. "I know you're opposed, but I should hire a nurse. You'll be returning to work soon, and—"

"I won't," I say with little inflection as I hand her an orange.

"What?" She looks confused.

"I won't be returning to work. I resigned after my mother tried to manipulate me into returning to work early and forgetting about my grief. I thought about Holt's plan to open his restaurant and realized life is too short to waste doing a job I hate when I have the luxury of a generous trust fund and time to figure out what'll make me happy." Bravely, I take her hand. "Whatever that is, I'm sure you'll be part of it."

Her eyes widen, and her cheeks darken slightly. "Of course. I'll be having your daughter." She sounds nervous, speaking in a high-pitched voice.

"That's not what I meant. I meant, I want to be a part of the baby's life, and I want you to be a part of my life. I don't know how that'll look, but I want to explore it. I like you, Jessica. I like you a lot, and I want to get to know you better. I want to spend time with you and the baby. I want to be a family." I take a deep breath, hoping I didn't scare her off.

"I like you too. A lot, which is crazy, because we barely got along before this, but I feel like we understand each other now." She meets my gaze. "I want to get to know you too. I want to explore this thing between us."

"Me too. I think it's worth exploring, don't you?" I raise her hand to my lips and kiss it, unable to resist. It's a poor substitute for her lips, but there's no way I'm rushing her. She's just agreed to let me into her life, and I don't want to mess that up.

"I do." She blushes again, and I wonder what she's thinking.

We finish eating, and then she takes a nap. While she sleeps, I call Tanner for legal help with my resignation and to see if I need to sever anything legally with Lara. We have some joint assets, and I'm not sure what needs to be done. He promises to come by the next day to discuss it.

Afterward, I sit in the living room and surf the Internet. My parents are in Europe for a merger meeting, so they're not an issue. Lara's parents are in town, but they haven't bothered to call me, so I don't bother to call them. She probably hasn't even told Chester and Alyce yet, and I can't blame her.

We need to talk to Holt's parents, but I'm sure Jessica isn't up to that today. While she's napping, I arrange for someone to pack up her bedroom and anything that looks important to bring to my place. Then I contact her landlord to let him know she'll be away for a while and pay the next three months of her rent to ensure she has a home to return to when she's off bed rest—though I hope she'll choose to stay with me.

By the time she wakes up, I've ordered lunch and arranged it on a tray. I carry it into her room and find her sitting on the bed, looking sleepy but adorable.

"Hey. Lunch is served." I put the tray down in front of her.

"Thank you. This looks amazing." She picks up the sandwich and takes a bite before frowning. "Ugh, mustard."

Her face is so adorable that I laugh. "In that case, why don't you have my roast beef dip, and I'll take the turkey? I forgot to ask if you liked mustard."

"I don't. It's gross. I prefer mayonnaise on my sandwiches." She swaps the plates and takes a big bite of the other sandwich. "Mmm. This is so good."

"Glad you like it." I watch her eat, fascinated by the way she licks the corner of her mouth to catch a drop of au jus. When she catches me staring, I blush and look away. "I'm glad you like it."

"I do. Thank you." She finishes her sandwich and starts on the fruit salad. "This is delicious. Did you make it?"

"Nope. I ordered it from the deli down the street along with the sandwiches." I grin. "I'm not that talented in the kitchen. Lara did most of the cooking."

"I'm not either. I can make a few things, but I usually order in or heat up something." She pops a grape into her mouth, making a soft noise of pleasure that makes my cock twitch.

"I'm not bad, but I'm not good either. I'm more of a grill guy. Give me a steak or some chicken, and I'm good to go." I lean back in the chair, watching her though I try not to be creepy about it. "Holt taught me some things when we shared an apartment with Tanner as undergrads."

She arches a brow. "You mean, you college boys didn't have a maid, housekeeper, gardener, and a chef?"

I flush but grin. "No landscape for a gardener."

"Ah, yes. The penthouse with a view of the city. I remember it well." She laughs. "I'm teasing. I'm not judging you. I'm just giving you a hard time. I'm really trying to let go of my low opinion of wealth, because let's be honest—I'd love being rich if I had the chance. Who wouldn't?"

I smile. "I think you'd probably do more with it than most people in my parents' social circle though. You care about others and would use your money to help them. Most of their friends are selfish and only care about themselves and their own comforts."

"I'm sure that's true, which is why I'm glad I'm not in that world. It seems like a lonely and shallow existence." She finishes the fruit salad and drinks the juice before leaning back against the pillows with a sigh. "That was good. Thank you."

"You're welcome, and it is." Seeing her frown, I say, "Lonely and shallow, I mean. I've spent thirty-one years conforming, but now...I need to figure out how to be me and be happy doing it."

"I'm sure you will. You're smart and kind. You'll find your path." She pats my arm. "I'm going to take a shower. I feel sticky after sleeping. Is that okay?"

I nod. "Of course. Take your time. I'll be here if you need anything."

She thanks me and disappears into the bathroom. I hear the shower turn on, and I imagine her naked body, glistening with water. My cock grows hard, and I groan. I'm going to be in serious trouble living with her.

I try to distract myself by cleaning up the dishes, but I keep hearing the sound of the water hitting her skin, and I can't get it out of my mind. I'm so turned on that I can't concentrate on anything else.

Finally, I give in and go to my room. I lock the door and pull down my pants, freeing my aching cock. I close my eyes and stroke it, imagining Jessica in the shower, lathering her breasts with soap. I picture myself joining her, taking over the task and massaging her slippery mounds before dropping to my knees to suck her nipples. She moans and grips my hair, pulling me closer as I lick and suck her.

I pump my cock harder, imagining her touching herself as I tease her nipples. She's soaking wet, and she pulls me to my feet. I push her against the wall, and she wraps her legs around my waist. I slide my cock into her tight, hot channel, and she cries out in pleasure. As I fuck her against the wall, she screams my name, begging me to go deeper. I thrust into her, pounding her harder and faster until she comes with a shuddering cry.

My orgasm rips through me, and I come hard, spurting into my hand. I grab a tissue from the nightstand and clean up before collapsing onto the bed. I feel guilty for fantasizing about her, but I can't help it. I want her so badly that I can barely control myself. I want to taste every inch of her body and bury my cock inside her. I want to make her scream my name as she comes.

As I lay there, I realize I'm falling for her, and I don't know what to do about it. I don't know if she feels the same way, or if she'll ever see me as anything other than Charlotte's father. At least she no longer hates me, so that's a start.

Chapter 10—Maddox

WE SETTLE INTO A ROUTINE over the next few days. I cook, we eat, and then she naps. Afterward, we hang out and talk. I learn a lot about her, and she learns a lot about me. We have a lot in common, and I enjoy spending time with her. She's funny, kind, and caring, and I can't help but fall more and more in love with her.

At night, I lie in bed and fantasize about her. I jerk off every night, imagining what it would be like to be with her. I want her so badly that it's driving me crazy. I know I can't rush her, but I'm not sure how much longer I can wait.

We're cuddling on my couch, and it's perfectly innocent, but my erection keeps forgetting that. I'm doing my best to hide it from her until she shifts as I'm reaching for the popcorn. Suddenly, her hand is across my bulge, and I freeze.

"Sorry." She jerks her hand away. "I didn't mean to touch you, I swear. I was just trying to reach the remote."

"It's okay. I don't mind. I'm just a little, uh, excited." I clear my throat.

"Excited? About the movie?" She glances at the screen, where two people are having sex.

"Not exactly." I shift my hips, and my erection presses against her thigh.

"Oh." She blushes and looks away. "I didn't realize you were, um, that interested in the movie."

"It's not the movie." I take her hand and place it on my cock. "It's you."

She stares at me, her eyes wide. "What?"

"You heard me. It's you. You're beautiful, and I'm attracted to you. I told you that, but you didn't seem to hear me."

She frowns. "I told you I wanted to see where things lead."

I laugh in a husky way. "So do I. He has some definite ideas about where it should lead."

She blushes and pulls away her hand. "I don't think that's a good idea. We're supposed to be co-parenting, not having a fling."

"Why can't we do both?" I lean in and kiss her neck.

She shivers and closes her eyes. "Because it'll complicate things."

"Maybe it'll simplify them." I nip at her earlobe.

"Maddox..." She trails off as I nibble on her neck.

"Jessica..." I mimic her tone. "Tell me you don't feel the same way, and I'll stop."

She whimpers when I trail kisses along her jawline. "I can't."

"Good." I capture her mouth in a searing kiss, my tongue sweeping in to claim hers. She tastes like honey and vanilla, and I can't get enough. I kiss her hungrily, devouring her lips and sucking on her tongue. She moans and clutches my shoulders, her nails digging into my skin.

I pull her onto my lap, so she's straddling me, and I grip her ass, grinding her against my throbbing cock. She gasps and breaks the kiss, panting. "Maddox, I can't. I'm on pelvic rest." She sounds genuinely regretful. "I can't have anything inside or have an orgasm."

I smirk. "That's not a problem. There's plenty I can do without penetrating you."

"Like what?" She sounds curious.

"Let me show you." I stand up with her in my arms and carry her to my bedroom. Since it wouldn't be fair to rev her up without giving her an orgasm, I rein in my urges and find some massage oil. "Strip," I say.

She hesitates but does as I ask, revealing her gorgeous body. I stare at her full breasts and curvy hips, my cock straining against my jeans. "Lay on your left side and get comfortable."

She does, and I kneel beside the bed, pouring some of the oil on her back. I rub it in, starting with her shoulders and working my way down her spine. "Did you know, there are some massage techniques you shouldn't use on a pregnant woman?"

She moans as I knead her muscles. "Um, no, but you sound like an expert."

"I did a little research. It's important to be careful when massaging a pregnant woman. You don't want to cause any harm to the mother or baby." I continue rubbing her back, moving to her buttocks. "For example, you can't use any deep pressure on the abdomen or uterus. Also, avoid using any oils that might irritate the skin or cause allergic reactions or contractions."

"Mmm, that feels so good." She sighs, her eyes closed.

I work my way down her thighs and calves, paying special attention to the soles of her feet. I've never had a foot fetish, but her luscious toes might change my mind. I force myself to keep this sensual, not sexual. "Massage can also help relieve some of the discomfort and pain associated with pregnancy. It can improve circulation, reduce swelling, and increase relaxation."

"I'll have to remember that. It's nice to be pampered." She smiles as I move to her other side and repeat the process.

We both freeze when my hands hover above her breasts. She looks indecisive before slowly thrusting out her chest, brushing her brown nipples against my palms. I swallow hard, fighting the urge to pinch them. Instead, I gently cup her breasts and massage them, avoiding the sensitive tips. She lets out a soft moan, and heat pools in my groin. I want her so badly that it hurts, but I have to be patient.

As I work my way down her body, I can't resist pressing my lips to the swell of her belly. I kiss it tenderly, whispering, "Hello, Charlotte. It's Daddy. I can't wait to meet you."

Jessica sniffles, and I glance up to see tears streaming down her cheeks. "I'm sorry. I'm not usually so emotional, but you caught me off guard."

"Don't apologize. I understand. This is a big deal. We're creating a life together. That's not something to take lightly." I kiss her belly again before continuing the massage.

When I finish, she's practically purring like a kitten. I stand up and stretch, my erection tenting my jeans. "I'm going to take a cold shower. Feel free to sleep in here tonight. I'll sleep on the couch."

She sits up, her eyes fixed on my crotch. "I'm on pelvic rest..."

I nod. "I know."

Jessica gives me a tempting smile. "You're not. Why don't I take care of that for you, since you took such good care of me?"

I blink. "Are you sure? I don't want to hurt you or the baby."

She nods. "I'm sure. Just be gentle, and we'll be fine."

I strip off my clothes and join her on the bed, kissing her deeply. Our tongues tangle, and I groan, my cock throbbing with need. She pushes me onto my back and straddles me, her wet slit pressed against my shaft for just a second. It's torture when she moves away, but she's trailing her tongue down my chest, so I'm stiff with need and anticipation.

Her fingers wrap around my cock, and she strokes it gently, teasing the tip with her thumb. I gasp, my hips bucking involuntarily. She smiles and continues stroking me, her hand moving up and down my length. I'm desperate for release, but I don't want to come too soon with her mouth getting ever closer.

Just when I think I can't take it anymore, her lips close around the head of my shaft, and I nearly explode. She sucks on it gently, her tongue swirling around the tip. I groan, my fingers tangling in her hair. She takes me deeper into her mouth, her tongue licking and teasing me. I'm lost in a haze of pleasure, my body trembling with desire.

I'm not sure how long she tortures me with her mouth, but eventually, she focuses on the head of my cock, sucking and licking it like a lollipop. I'm on the verge of coming, and I warn her. "I'm going to come."

She doesn't stop, and I explode, filling her mouth with my seed. She swallows it all, her tongue still working its magic on my cock. I'm shaking with the intensity of my release, and I collapse on the bed, spent.

"Holy hell, that was incredible." I pant.

She grins. "Glad you enjoyed it."

"Enjoyed it? That's an understatement. I think I saw stars." I pull her close and kiss her, tasting myself on her lips. "I feel like a selfish bastard, not being able to make you come."

She giggles. "It's okay. It's not like you can penetrate me, and I can't have an orgasm. This was the next best thing, and your massage made me feel amazing."

"I'm glad. I wanted to make you feel good. You deserve it." I kiss her again, savoring the taste of her lips. "Shower with me?"

She agrees, and we shower together, soaping each other up and rinsing off. It's a sweet and intimate experience, and I love every minute of it. Afterward, I dry her off and comb her thick curls. She laughs, saying, "It's going to be awful by the time I'm able to get to the salon."

"I like it." I run my fingers through the thick locks. "I didn't realize how long your hair was."

She nods. "My hair dries tight. Maybe I'll cut it all off before the baby comes."

I feign a pout. "It's your hair, but I hope you won't."

"We'll see. It depends on how much energy I have." She yawns. "I'm tired."

"Me too." I hesitate, not wanting to rush her, but it doesn't feel that extreme after our intimate bonding. "Do you want to sleep with me tonight? In my bed?"

She bites her lip. "I do, but I don't want to tempt you. I can't have sex, and you're a very virile man." Jessica grins. "I'm afraid of tempting myself too."

I put an arm around her. "We're not going to do anything to hurt Charlotte, and I just want to hold you. That's all. I promise. I'm not expecting anything more."

She snuggles against me. "Okay. I trust you. I just hope I can trust myself."

We climb into bed, and I spoon her, holding her close. I can almost hear her thinking in the darkness. "Your thoughts are keeping me awake," I tease gently.

She sighs, shifting in my arms. "Are we making a mistake? If this thing implodes, it's going to be so much harder to co-parent."

"We're adults. We'll figure it out, but I don't think it'll implode. I think we have a connection, and we have a baby. That's a pretty solid foundation for a relationship, don't you think?" I nuzzle her hair, breathing in the scent of her shampoo.

"I guess. I just worry. I don't want to lose you. I don't want to lose this baby. I've already lost so much." Her voice cracks.

"I know, but I think it's worth the risk. Why settle for okay when we could have incredible?" I kiss her shoulder.

"I'm scared. I'm not used to feeling this way. I'm used to being in control of my life, and now, I'm not. Everything is out of my control. I feel like I'm on a rollercoaster ride, and I can't get off." She sounds miserable.

"I know. I feel the same way, but I think it's worth it. I think we're worth it." I turn her to face me, kissing her gently. "I'm not going anywhere. I'm right here with you, and I'm not letting you go."

She smiles and kisses me back. "I'm glad. You make me feel safe."

"Good. That's what I want. Now, let's get some sleep. We have a busy day of watching movies tomorrow." I roll onto my back and pull her into my arms.

She laughs as she rests her head on my chest and falls asleep. I follow soon after, content and happy for the first time in a long time. I have no doubts or regrets, and though she probably does, I'm determined to help her conquer them, because I want her to love me as much as I love her.

I'm almost asleep when I have the thought, and my eyes snap open. Do I love her? Is that why I'm so drawn to her?

I consider it for a moment before deciding that I do. I love her. I'm in love with her. I'm not sure when it happened, but it did, and I'm not going to fight it. I'm going to embrace it and hope she loves me too.

THE NEXT MORNING, WE wake tangled together, and I kiss her good morning. "How do you feel?"

"Good. A little hungry." She stretches. "Is that bacon I smell?"

"It could be." I laugh at her hint and roll out of bed. "Do you feel like coming to the kitchen, or do you want me to bring a tray?"

She looks a bit grumpy. "I feel like going for a ten-mile run, and I don't even jog. I'm sick of being cooped up, but it's for a worthy cause." She places her hand on her belly. "I'll come to the kitchen after I get dressed. I think that's close enough to bed rest. I need to get up and move around."

"Fair enough. I'll see you in a few minutes." I dress in a pair of sweatpants and a T-shirt before heading to the kitchen. I'm scrambling eggs and frying bacon when the doorbell rings.

I answer it to find Tanner standing there with his briefcase. "Hey, man. Come on in. Jessica's on her way to the kitchen."

He follows me in and sets his briefcase on the counter. "I'm here to help you with whatever you need. What's on the agenda today?"

I shrug. "Nothing really. We're just hanging out. Jessica's on bed rest, so I'm trying to keep her entertained. We're going to watch a movie after breakfast. Want to join us?"

Tanner shakes his head. "No, thanks. I have a lot of work to do. I'm going to set up in your office so we can go over the documents I'm going to file with your former company. Also, Lara got back to me already and told me she's fine with letting me divide everything between us. She trusts my judgment and insists anything that isn't equal should go to you, since you're unemployed with a baby on the way." He grins at that zinger.

I chuckle. "Thanks, man. I appreciate it. I'll have to dip into the trust fund so I can pay your exorbitant services."

Tanner nods. "They're outrageous, aren't they? When I'm partner...I'll probably raise them even more." He winks at me.

"Do you want breakfast?" I ask him as I hear Jessica approaching.

"No, thanks. I ate before I came." He glances over and does a double take. "Jessica, hi. How are you?" He grins. "You've suddenly popped."

She blushes. "I have. I'm not sure if it's the baby or the fact that I haven't been able to exercise. I'm hoping for the former." She smiles. "It's nice to see you again. Thank you for helping Maddox with the legal stuff."

He waves a hand. "It's no problem. I'm happy to help. I'm going to get to work. You guys enjoy breakfast. I'll be in the office when you're done." He picks up his briefcase and heads down the hall.

I serve Jessica a plate of food, and we sit down to eat. She digs in, moaning with pleasure. "This is delicious. I'm starving."

I grin. "The nutritionist told me to put protein powder in the eggs. I thought it'd be weird, but it works. They're fluffy and tasty."

"I can tell. They're great." She finishes her plate and leans back, patting her stomach. "That was so good. I'm stuffed."

"Want to go pick out a movie, and I'll join you as soon as I'm done with Tanner?" I suggest.

She nods. "Sure. I'm going to grab a glass of milk. Can I get you anything?"

I shake my head. "I'm good. Thanks." I watch her walk away, admiring the view. She's wearing a loose-fitting maternity top and a pair of leggings, but she's still sexy as hell.

After she leaves, I clean up the dishes and head to my office. Tanner is sitting at the desk, tapping away on his laptop. "I've drafted a few different agreements that we can use to dissolve your shares of the company. I'm just finishing up the last one, and then I'll print them out so you can look them over."

"Sounds good. I trust you." I sink into the chair across from him.

"I know, but it's important that you read them and make sure you're comfortable with what they say. Never trust an attorney." He grins as he gives the advice. "Trust me."

I roll my eyes and laugh, soon reading and signing off on everything. We're nearly done when my doorbell rings. "Hold that thought."

"I'll be here."

I hurry into the living room, coming to an abrupt halt at the sight of Andrew and Hilary McEntire standing in the foyer, staring at Jessica, who has opened the door for them.

Chapter 11—Jessica

I'VE JUST SETTLED ON a movie I think Maddox and I will both like when the doorbell rings. I pause the TV and frown, wondering who it could be. I'm not expecting anyone, and I doubt Maddox is either.

I make my way to the front door and open it, surprised to find Andrew and Hilary McEntire on the other side. I instantly recognize Holt's parents. I never really socialized with them, but I was part of their wedding—despite Hilary's best efforts for the photographer to maneuver me out of the wedding photos since my skin was too dark to match the others in the photos—so I know who they are.

"Hello, Mr. and Mrs. McEntire. How are you?" I greet them politely, though I'm not sure why they're here.

Andrew's gaze sweeps over me, and he frowns. "Who are you, and where is Maddox?"

"I'm Jessica Malone." I grit my teeth, sure Hilary recognizes me from the glimmer in her eyes, but she makes no acknowledgement of that. "I'm the one carrying..." I trail off, not sure how to finish that, since this baby would have been Holt's if he hadn't died, but biologically, she's Maddox's.

"Beverly and Andrew, how unexpected," says Maddox from behind me. I turn to him as he comes forward, putting a bracing hand on my lower back. "What brings you by?"

Andrew gestures at me. "Your father told me some alarming news, and I came by to discuss it with you."

"But not to discuss your grief over losing Holt?" he asks, voice tight.

Hilary sniffles, dabbing at her eyes with a lace handkerchief. "Of course, we're grieving, but we have to be strong. For the baby. We have to make sure this baby is taken care of and given the life she deserves, but we've lost track of her surrogate..." Her words trail off as she stares at my belly. "Why, is that you, Janessa?"

"Jessica." I keep the tone civil. "And yes, I'm the surrogate. I'm carrying the baby for Holt and Anya."

Andrew's brows shoot up. "Anya? My son's wife?"

Hilary sighs. "I told you about that unfortunate business, dear. When the girl couldn't stay pregnant, she asked her friend to have her baby for her."

Andrew grunts. "They should have just listened to the message nature was sending. She wasn't meant to have our grandchild." He glares at me now. "And neither were you, but here we are. I suppose we'll have to take responsibility for the infant once it's born and never mention the sordidness of its origins."

I glare at him. "Assisted reproductive technology is hardly seedy, Drew." His eyes narrow at that, which gives me a surge of pleasure. I refuse to offer fake respect to the man who made one of my best friends miserable. "I'm sure you wouldn't have objected to them using ART if Anya's pedigree was as long as her arm. She was a wonderful woman, and she and Holt would have been terrific parents. As for the baby, she's a Tillman, not a McEntire, and she'll be raised with love and support from her father and me. That's all she'll ever need."

Maddox hisses slightly, and I realize I just blurted out that information. I give him a small look of apology, but he just shrugs. "Yes, we're raising the baby together."

"You can't do that," Hilary protests. "She's a McEntire. She has a duty to her family and her heritage. You can't take her from us. We're her grandparents."

He shakes his head. "I'm not taking your granddaughter from you. You can visit her anytime you like, but she's staying with me. I'm her father, and I'm not giving her up. Not for anything. Jessica and I are committed to raising her together, and that's final."

Hilary is clearly confused. "How can you be the father? She's Holt's and that girl's."

Maddox glares at her. "That girl had a name. Anya, and it was your loss not giving her a chance. As for why I'm the father, Andrew wasn't able to produce sperm, so I donated for the conception."

Andrew looks horrified. "They were going to raise your child as theirs and not tell anyone? I would have passed on my fortune to a cuckoo in the nest. I can't believe it." He turns to Hilary. "I'm not supporting this farce of a pregnancy. The baby isn't our grandchild, and I won't claim her. I promised Philip I'd speak to you, but it's clear you're on a path no one can avert you from, Maddox. Regain control before you lose everything."

He doesn't bother looking at or speaking to me as he turns and storms out. Hilary hesitates for a moment, looking regretful. "I wanted to be a grandmother."

I feel some pity for her. "You still can. Holt was her father in every way that matters and would have raised her if he hadn't died. She's not biologically related, but she'll need grandparents." I touch my belly. "I'm not biologically related to her, but I already love her. It'll be the same for you."

Maddox nods. "If you want to be in her life, you can, but we're not giving her up. We're not giving her any reason to doubt how much she's loved and wanted. She's ours, and we're hers."

Hilary sighs. "I appreciate it, but that's not how we do things." With a shake of her head, she's back to an ice queen. "I don't expect I'll see you again, so I hope you have a healthy pregnancy and delivery, Janessa." She looks at Maddox. "Think carefully, son. Holt was so close to you that you were almost like a son of mine. I want you to find your way back to what matters."

"I have, and it means stepping back from what doesn't." He rests his hand on my belly as he nods to her. "Goodbye, Hilary."

She walks away, leaving us alone. I lean against him, and he wraps his arms around me. "That was intense."

"I'm sorry I blurted that out. I shouldn't have said it without talking to you first, but it seemed like the right thing to say in the moment." I glance up at him. "Are you angry with me?"

He kisses my forehead. "Not at all. I was going to tell them anyway. I was planning to tell Holt's parents as soon as you were off bed rest, so we could talk to them together." He looks worried then. "Are you stressed? Do you need to lie down?"

I shake my head. "I'm okay. I'm just a little shaken. I didn't expect that."

"Neither did I." He helps me to the couch and sits beside me. "I'm sorry you had to deal with that. Let me finish with Tanner, and we'll spend the rest of the day ignoring the world. Sound good?"

I nod. "Sounds perfect."

He goes to his office, and I curl up on the couch, pulling a throw blanket over myself. I'm still reeling from the encounter, but I'm also relieved. Maddox is on my side, and I'm glad Holt's cold and proper parents won't try to make any claim to Charlotte, even though I think they're stupid for their reasons choosing not to do so.

I'm not sure what the future holds, but I have a feeling it's going to be good, and I can't wait to see where it leads.

A FEW HOURS LATER, we're curled up together on the couch, watching a romantic comedy, when my phone buzzes. I lean forward and say, "A reminder for my appointment with Willow tomorrow." I lick my lips, hoping not to tease him too much. "I haven't had any further bleeding, so if the placenta has moved, I'll probably be off bed rest...and pelvic rest."

His eyes heat as he looks at me. "Is that right? So, you could start moving around more?"

I nod. "I could. I could also do other activities, like riding a...horse."

"Riding a horse?" He sounds amused. "I didn't know you rode horses."

"I don't, but I'm willing to learn."

His eyes are full of lust. "That's very generous of you."

"I'll have to practice on something else though. It's not safe for a pregnant woman to ride a horse." I lick my lips again. "Something smaller, maybe?"

He chuckles. "I think I might have just the thing. Not much smaller, you understand?"

I laugh, leaning in to kiss him. "I hope so, because I'm really horny."

He groans. "Don't say that. I can't do anything with you. I can't penetrate you until after the appointment tomorrow. Maybe." He groans again. "The next twenty weeks are going to kill me if you're still restricted."

I laugh, but it's strained. "Me too. You have no idea how the hormones rage in the second trimester."

He raises a brow. "Really? That's interesting."

"It is, and it's not. I feel like I'm going crazy with desire, but I can't act on it." I sigh. "I know it's for Charlotte's safety, but it's hard."

"I bet." He nuzzles my neck. "I wish there was something I could do to help, but I don't know what."

I close my eyes, enjoying the sensation of his lips on my skin. "Just keep doing that." With a sigh, I pull away. "On second thought, don't, because it makes it harder to maintain control."

"I'm hoping for good news tomorrow." His neck is taut as he says that, and he's clearly clinging to his last thread of control.

So am I.

"HELLO," SAYS WILLOW when she enters the exam room the next afternoon. "How are we feeling?"

"Better. No more spotting, and the cramping has stopped, so I'm hoping that means the placenta has moved." I smile at her. "I'm ready to get off bed rest." And pelvic rest.

She nods as she pulls on a pair of gloves. "Let's see what we've got, shall we?"

I lift my shirt and lower my pants, and she begins the examination. I hold my breath as she checks the position of the placenta and Charlotte.

"Let's get a quick ultrasound to confirm where the placenta is, but I think it's moving up nicely. It's definitely not in the lower half anymore, and there's no sign of separation, so that's very good news." She walks to the corner to retrieve the ultrasound and rolls it back to the bed.

Maddox leans closer, clearly wanting to see her again. So do I.

Willow squirts the gel onto my belly and starts to move the wand. "There she is. She's got a nice strong heartbeat."

We both stare at the screen, mesmerized by the sight of our daughter. Maddox reaches for my hand and squeezes it. "She's so beautiful."

I nod, unable to speak. I'm so overwhelmed with emotion that I can barely breathe.

"She's perfect," says Willow. "I'm going to check the position of the placenta, and then we'll go from there." She moves the wand, and her eyes widen. "Oh, wow. It's almost completely moved. It's just hanging in the upper part of the uterus, but it's not touching the cervix anymore. I think you're safe to resume normal activity." She smiles. "Congratulations, Mom and Dad."

Tears fill my eyes, and I squeeze his hand. "Thank you, Willow."

Maddox clears his throat. "Can we see her again?"

"Of course." She repositions the wand and shows us the baby again. "I can print out a picture for you to take home if you like."

"Please," he says. "Two, if you can."

I laugh. "I think we're going to need more than two, but that's a good start."

"I'll make sure you get a set of four." She prints out the pictures and hands them to us. "I'll let you get dressed, and I'll schedule your next appointment. Take care, and congratulations."

"Thank you, Willow." I beam at Maddox as she leaves the room. "This is amazing."

"It is." He presses a kiss to my forehead. "I'm so happy."

I grin as I sit up and reach for my clothes. "Me too. Now, let's go home and celebrate."

He laughs. "I like the way you think."

We leave the midwife's office and drive home. Once inside, I strip off my clothes as I walk to the bedroom, knowing he's following.

"Do you want to go out for dinner? I know you're stir-crazy."

I smile as I unfasten my bra. "Sounds good...later. Right now, I want to stay in and celebrate with you."

"I can't argue with that." He strips off his own clothes and joins me in the bed.

I roll to face him, smiling as his hand cups my cheek. "Hi."

He grins. "Hi, yourself. Are you ready to play?"

I nod. "I'm more than ready. I've been dreaming about this for days."

"Me too." He leans in and kisses me, his tongue sweeping into my mouth.

I moan and press closer to him, reveling in the feel of his warm, naked body against mine. He's hard and ready, and I can't wait to feel him inside me.

We kiss, exploring each other's mouths as our hands roam over each other's bodies. It's been a long time since I've had a lover, and I've been panting for him for days, if not longer. For an instant, it feels strange to so strongly desire the man I used to despise, but he's different now, and so am I.

I stare into his eyes for a long moment, losing myself in the bright blue pools of his irises. His gaze is filled with hunger and desire, and excitement courses through me at the knowledge that he wants me as much as I want him.

"I need you," I whisper, my voice thick with passion.

He nods, his expression mirroring my own. "I need you too."

Our lips meet again in a kiss of fire and urgency, our tongues tangling as our hands explore. I run my fingers down his chest, tracing the lines of his muscles and feeling the strength of his body. He's solid and powerful, and I can't wait to feel him inside me.

He cups my breasts, teasing my sensitive nipples with his thumbs. I arch into his touch, moaning softly as pleasure ripples through me. I've never felt this way before, so desperate and aching with need. I've never needed a man like I need him right now.

He kisses his way down my neck, nibbling and sucking on my skin as he goes. I gasp and writhe beneath him, my body on fire with desire. I'm already wet and throbbing.

He trails his hand down my belly, pausing to caress my swollen mound while lightly sucking one of my nipples. I cry out in ecstasy, my hips bucking as I seek relief from the sweet torment. "Please," I beg, my voice hoarse with longing. "I can't take it anymore. I need you."

He nods, his breathing ragged as he slips a finger into my slick folds. I groan as he strokes my clit, sending waves of pleasure coursing through my body. He slides another finger into me, and I grip the sheets, my toes curling as I teeter on the edge of release.

"So wet." He presses lightly. "I want to taste your nectar."

I whimper as he withdraws his fingers and licks them clean. "You taste so good." He lowers his head between my legs, teasing my clit with his tongue.

I gasp and shudder, my entire body trembling with need. I'm dizzy with desire, and I can't think straight. All I can focus on is the exquisite sensations he's creating deep within me.

He laps at my juices, humming in delight as he feasts on my core. I cry out, gripping his hair as I grind against his face, seeking more friction. He sucks on my clit, making me see stars. I'm close to coming, and I can't hold back any longer.

"Maddox," I scream, my body convulsing as my orgasm crashes over me.

He continues to suck and lick me through my climax, drawing out my pleasure until I'm spent and gasping for air. I collapse against the pillows, my limbs shaking from the intensity of my release.

He looks up at me, grinning. "You're so sexy when you come."

I smile, my cheeks flushed with pleasure. "That was incredible."

He crawls up my body, kissing me deeply. I can taste my own arousal on his lips, and it only fuels my desire for him. I wrap my arms around his neck, pulling him closer as I deepen the kiss.

He positions himself on his back, and I straddle him, eager to take him inside me. I'm still throbbing and needy, and I can't wait any longer. I guide his cock to my entrance, sinking down on him with a moan of satisfaction.

He grips my hips, thrusting up into me as I ride him. Our bodies move in perfect harmony, our shared passion building to a fever pitch. I can feel another orgasm approaching, and I chase it, grinding down on his shaft as he pumps into me.

"You feel so good," he says, his voice husky with desire. "I love being inside you."

I nod, unable to form words as I lose myself in the moment. The pressure is building, and I'm close to coming again. He reaches between us, stroking my clit as I rock on top of him.

"Come for me, baby," he urges, his eyes locked on mine. "I want to feel you come undone around me."

His words send me over the edge, and I cry out as my climax hits, my inner walls clenching around him. He groans, his own release following shortly after. We ride out the waves of pleasure together, our bodies entwined as we bask in the afterglow.

I collapse against his chest, utterly spent and satisfied. I've never experienced anything like that before, and I'll never forget it.

"That was worth the wait." I giggle, feeling giddy.

He grins. "I agree." He runs a hand up and down my back, sending shivers of pleasure through me. "Ready for round two?"

I laugh. "Give me a few minutes to recover, and I'll be ready for anything."

He shakes his head. "Certain positions are less safe right now."

I prop my head on my hand and look at him. "I know, but I think it's wonderful that you do too. I've seen you reading the baby books and pregnancy books on your phone. I appreciate your enthusiasm."

He looks embarrassed for a moment before pulling me closer for another kiss. "I'm enthusiastic about all kinds of things. Like the fact that I'm starving. Want to go out for dinner?"

I nod. "I'd love to...after round two."

He laughs. "I like the way you think."

We spend the rest of the evening celebrating our newfound freedom and enjoying each other's company. By the end of the night, I'm exhausted but happier than I've been in a long time, and we never do make it to the restaurant, but I don't care.

Chapter 12—Maddox

THE NEXT FEW DAYS ARE a contented haze of sex and bonding, and I could happily spend the rest of my life doing nothing but exploring—sex and the city now that she's no longer on bed rest—but a call from Lara drags me out of our blissful bubble Saturday evening.

"Hey," I say, putting her on speakerphone while Jessica is fixing a light dinner of stir fry, insisting on pampering me for a change. "How are things going with Felipe?"

She sighs. "Not great. He's been in rehab for a week, and he's not responding well to the treatment. They're talking about releasing him early, and I'm afraid he's going to relapse as soon as he gets out, but he thinks we should rent a private island and stay there for a while, away from temptation."

"Are you safe if you do that?" I ask, suddenly worried what he might do if he relapses.

"I think so. He's been sober since he went in, and he seems to be doing better, but I'm not sure what to do. He wants me to go with him, but I can't abandon my job and my life here...especially since we have breakfast scheduled with both our parents tomorrow."

I groan. "Oh. I haven't spoken to mine in weeks. Have you told them we broke up?"

She hesitates. "Not that, no. Will you please come tomorrow, so we can tell them together?"

"Lara, I'm sorry, but I can't. I'm in the middle of something important, and I can't drop everything to—"

"I'll be fine for a couple of hours," says Jessica cheerfully, like she's helping. Dammit.

I glare at her. "No, you won't."

She raises her eyebrows. "Yes, I will. You can go. It's okay."

Lara snorts. "Who is that?"

"Jessica."

"Is she still on bed rest?" asks Lara.

"No," says Jessica, giving me an encouraging look. "He's available to help break the news."

"I don't want to see my parents," I say bluntly, clearly to both of them, since Jessica is now talking too.

She puts down the chopsticks to hug me. "I know, but you should get it over with." With a kiss, she returns to the stove.

Lara laughs. "I like her. She speaks sense. Please come, Maddox. I need you."

I sigh. "Fine. What time do you want me there?"

"Breakfast is at nine-fifteen. Can you meet me at eight-forty-five at the coffee shop across the street from my apartment? We're meeting them at the Ritz. I picked neutral ground when I set it up, because you know how our mothers subtly compete about everything."

"'What a charming little vase. I'll have to ask my decorator if she knows where to find such a bargain,'" I say falsetto, making Lara laugh and Jessica grin.

"Exactly. So, eight-forty-five, and thank you. I owe you one, Maddox."

"Yeah, you do." I hang up and turn to Jessica. "Why did you do that?"

She turns off the burner and comes to give me a hug. "Because she needs you, and you need to get it over with."

"I hate my parents. They're always judging everything I do."

She kisses me gently. "I know, but they're your family, and they must love you. Surely, they'll want to know you're making them grandparents."

"They'll want to know why I knocked up a stranger and ruined my relationship with Lara. That's what they'll care about."

She hugs me tighter. "Then show them what a good father you'll be. Show them how happy you are, and make sure they know the full story about the knocking-up. That you'd never touched me before the pregnancy."

I growl low in my throat, capturing her lips for a deep kiss. "I can't claim that now."

She smiles against my lips. "No, but you can tell them the truth about us."

I pull her closer, sliding my hands under her shirt. "I could, but they'll just judge me for it."

Her eyes sparkle. "Then make them jealous. Tell them how much fun we're having, and how you're learning to cook and clean since I fired the housekeeping service. They'll have to admit you're not the spoiled rich boy they expect you to be."

I chuckle. "That would probably actually kill them from the shock. A Tillman doesn't do manual labor." I roll my eyes. "Will you come with me?"

She hesitates before shaking her head. "I think you'd be better off facing this with Lara and letting me meet them at a less charged time. I mean, if you really need me…" She's clearly torn.

I shake my head. "I can handle it. I just wanted you to know you're welcome. They're not going to be happy with or for me."

"I'm sure they'll understand once you explain everything." She gives me a final squeeze. "Now, let's eat, and then you can take me to the movies. I've been dying to see the new action flick."

I wish I were as optimistic as Jessica, but I know my folks, and it's not going to be that easy.

LARA AND I ENTER THE restaurant at the Ritz promptly at nine-fourteen, and I see her parents sitting with mine at a large corner table. My parents appear to be arguing with hers, but they stop as soon as they spot us.

"There you are," says Viv, rising to greet us. "We were starting to worry."

Chester glowers at me. "You're late, Maddox."

I ignore her father's words.

"Sorry, Mother. It was my fault. I was running behind." Lara gives her mother a quick hug before greeting Viv.

My father rises to his feet to embrace me perfunctorily. "Good to see you, son. We were just discussing how we can resolve this unfortunate situation with the Briggs."

I frown. "What situation?"

Philip rolls his eyes. "Don't play dumb, Maddox. You know exactly what I'm referring to. You can't resign without expecting a response, and surely, Lara can talk some sense into you."

I stiffen. "I'm not here to discuss resigning, and I won't change my mind about that."

"Of course, you will," says my mom, patting my arm. "Once you get this nonsense out of your system, you'll see how ridiculous it is. Now, sit down and have a mimosa. There's plenty of time to discuss this later."

I grit my teeth. "I'm not changing my mind, and I'm not drinking."

"Please listen to Viv," says Alyce. "Hilary McEntire told me the most upsetting thing, and you have to assure us it isn't true."

That gets my parents' attention, and Lara and I both collapse into seats at roughly the same time. I hadn't expected any of them to know a thing about the baby being mine before we broke the news.

"What has Hilary said?" asks my mother, her expression concerned.

Alyce's eyes narrow. "She said Holt's wife's surrogate is pregnant with Maddox's child. Is that true?"

Lara and I exchange a glance, and I reach for her hand in a friendly way. "It's true. Holt and Anya asked me to be a sperm donor for their surrogate, and I agreed. They died in a car accident, and I'm the baby's biological father. I intend to raise the child with the surrogate, Jessica, and be a part of the baby's life."

Chester's jaw drops. "You can't be serious. This is a joke, right?"

I shake my head. "I'm completely serious. Jessica and I are in a relationship, and we plan to raise the baby together."

"This is preposterous," snaps my father. "You're marrying my daughter, so how are you carrying on with some surrogate who isn't our kind?"

Lara jumps to her feet. "I'm not marrying Maddox. And I hope you're not implying what I think you're implying about Jessica."

Viv pats her shoulder. "Calm down, dear. Your father didn't mean it that way."

"The hell I didn't, Viv," says Chester. "It's obvious she's not our kind. Surely, she'll take the child if you offer her enough, Maddox."

He completely ignores Lara's news that we aren't getting married. I'm not sure what to address first. "Jessica isn't interested in money, and the baby is mine, as well as hers. I intend to honor my commitment to Holt and Anya, and Jessica and I are raising the baby together. The baby will be a Tillman, and I'm prepared to acknowledge that publicly."

"You can't possibly be considering this," says Philip, looking horrified. "Your grandfather would be turning in his grave."

"Grandfather was a racist bastard, who hated anyone who wasn't white or wealthy," I say harshly. "I'm not ashamed of my child, and I'm not abandoning my responsibility as a father."

"Now, Philip, calm down. The surrogate didn't contribute any DNA. If Maddox insists on acknowledging the child, the mother was Anya. Right?" My mother turns to look at me as she asks.

"Biologically, but since Anya is gone, Jessica is her mother."

"But not...racially," says my mother with every appearance of being delicate.

Lara makes a disgusted sound. "Viv, you're being terrible. I'm sure Jessica is a lovely person, and I support Maddox's decision to raise his child."

Her mother looks relieved. "Wonderful. You'll be her mother, and no one needs to know the sordid history. And you always said you wouldn't have children." Alyce looks like she might cry. "The next one will be our real grandchild, but we'll be sure to treat the first one well too, in honor of Maddox."

I'm getting progressively more disgusted, and Lara seems on the verge of exploding too. "Mother, Jessica is the baby's mother. She's the one who will have carried her for nine months and given birth to her. She's the one who will feed her and comfort her in the middle of the night. She's the one who will teach her to walk and talk and ride a bike. I have no interest in any of those milestones with anyone's child, including my own."

"How can you support Maddox and not be involved with his child? Will this Jessica be the nanny?" My mother looks even more confused.

"Enough. Lara and I broke up." I make the announcement loudly enough to get the attention of the tables around us, which makes everyone else at the table fidget, but I don't care.

"Maddox, don't be foolish. Of course, you didn't. It's the stress of the surrogate's pregnancy. Once the baby is born, everything will be back to normal," says my mother. "We'll have a private adoption arranged for Lara, and no one will ever know a thing. The McEntires won't be able to complain, and you can go back to your life as usual."

"No," says my father. "The surrogate can have it. We'll write her a big check and send her away. Someone like her will be happy to have that kind of money."

"Undoubtedly," says Chester. "I'll contribute half just to make this mess disappear."

Lara gasps. "Daddy, how can you say that? Jessica is a wonderful person who is using her body to grow someone else's baby. That's pretty selfless. She isn't trying to extort money from Maddox."

"Surely, she is. Why else would she agree to have a baby for strangers?" Alyce looks at her husband for confirmation.

"They weren't strangers. Anya was like her sister," says Lara.

My father frowns. "I don't recall Holt's wife looking black."

I'm pleased at how hard Lara is fighting for me, though it's also for herself and her right to be with Felipe. She lets out a sound of aggravation. "I don't love Maddox. I never have, and I never will. He's not the man for me, and I refuse to be part of this farce. I'm in love with someone else, and I'm moving to Mexico City to be with him." She looks defiant when she adds, "Because Felipe is Hispanic."

"Felipe Morney?" asks Viv, her eyes wide.

Lara nods. "Yes, and I'm leaving the country with him. I'm not coming back, and I'm not seeing Maddox again."

"I'm afraid you'll have to," says her father coldly. "If you leave the country with him, you'll be cut off, Lara. No money, no connections, nothing."

"I have my own money, and I've made my own connections. I don't need anything from either of you." Her chin is high, and she looks like she means it.

"You're making a mistake, Lara. Felipe Morney is a drug addict and a criminal. He's not a suitable match for you. His band is terrible, and he's a disgrace to his family." Viv looks like she's about to start crying. "How can you do this to us?"

"And how can you disgrace us like this?" wails my mother.

I exchange a look with Lara as we both roll our eyes. "I'll call you tomorrow, Lara, and we'll figure out the details of the press release. I'm not giving up the baby. It's the only thing I have left of Holt and Anya, and I intend to be the father they wanted me to be."

Lara nods. "I understand, and I'm sure Jessica does too. She's seems like a wonderful woman, and she'll make a great mother."

"Thank you. I appreciate your support, and I'm sorry things didn't work out between us." Our parents are shouting in the background, suddenly uncaring about attracting attention, as we share a quick hand squeeze and rise together.

"Me too. Good luck, and I hope you're very happy with Jessica."

"I hope you find happiness with Felipe. Take care, Lara." With that, we turn and walk out of the restaurant, leaving our parents behind.

"That went well," I say dryly as we exit the building.

She laughs. "Not really, but at least they know now. I'm glad I finally told them how I feel about you. I'm tired of pretending."

"I'm sorry it took this for you to realize you're in love with Felipe and not with me. I wish we'd had the courage to be honest sooner." I lift my hand to hail a taxi. "Are you okay getting home, or would you like me to walk you?"

She shakes her head. "It's four blocks. I'll be fine. Have a good day, Maddox. I'll text you later."

"Okay, and thanks for everything. I'll call you tomorrow."

She waves and heads down the sidewalk, while I stand there watching her go. There are no lingering emotions or a tug of regret. She's back to being a friend, like a sister, as she always should have remained.

I'm free. Free to pursue Jessica and the baby. Free to live my life the way I want to. Free to make my own decisions and choices.

Free to be the father I was meant to be. And maybe a husband too, if things go as I expect.

I smile as I climb into the cab and give the driver the address. I can't wait to see Jessica and tell her about the morning's events, to hold her in my arms and kiss her. I can't wait to spend the rest of the day with her.

I can't wait to be with the woman I love.

Chapter 13—Jessica

I'M A LITTLE NERVOUS as I wait for his return. I know it's ridiculous, but part of me worries he and Lara's parents, as a combined force, will be enough to compel them back together. That'll be the end of our fairytale, and the thought is devastating.

I sink to the couch as I realize I'm falling in love with him. It's crazy and terrifying, but it's also exhilarating and exciting. I want to shout it from the rooftops, but I also want to keep it to myself because it's so precious and fragile.

I want to protect it and nurture it, and I want to see where it goes, but I'm also scared. What if he decides he doesn't want to be a part of the baby's life after all? What if he realizes he's still in love with Lara?

I'm a bundle of nerves by the time I hear his key in the lock, and I jump to my feet, heart racing. He enters the apartment with a huge grin on his face, and I rush toward him, throwing myself into his arms.

"Hey, hey, what's wrong?" He holds me tightly, stroking my hair.

"I was worried about you." I burrow against his chest, inhaling his scent.

"Why? I was only gone a couple of hours." He sounds amused.

I pull away to glare at him. "A lot can happen in a couple of hours. Did you and Lara get back together?"

He chuckles. "No, we did not. In fact, she told everyone she's in love with Felipe Morney and is moving to Mexico City with him."

I gasp. "Really? She's in love with the rockstar?"

"Yep, and he's apparently in love with her, as well. Their main problem is his addiction, but he's trying, and she's fighting for them." He smiles after a moment. "She fought for us too. She defended me and you and the baby to our parents. It was pretty amazing."

"Wow, that's great. I'm so happy for her." I'm also relieved beyond measure that they haven't gotten back together. "So, are you okay?"

He nods. "I am. It's weird, but I'm actually really okay. I don't care about my parents' opinion or the Briggs', for that matter. All I care about is you and Charlotte. I want to be with you and be a father to our daughter. I want to build a life with you and make you happy. I want to make you laugh and smile, and I want to make love to you whenever you want me to."

Relief overtakes me, and I sink against him. "Now sounds good."

He chuckles. "I'm serious, Jessica. I'm falling in love with you, and I want to be with you. I want to be there when you have the baby, and I want to raise her with you. I want to be there for all the doctor's appointments and Lamaze classes, and I want to be by your—"

I cut him off with a kiss. "I know, and I want all that too, but right now, I want *you*."

He groans. "You're killing me, woman. I'm trying to tell you how I feel, and you're distracting me with sex."

I laugh as I pull him down the hallway. "I'm just speeding up the process. Talk as you undress. We can do both at the same time."

He grumbles but follows me to the bedroom, and he starts talking as he strips off his clothes. "I'm falling in love with you, and I want to be with you forever. I want to marry you and raise Charlotte with you. I want us to be a family, and I want to give you the world."

I pause in removing my skirt to stare at him. "Maddox, are you proposing to me?"

He blinks. "I guess I am. Is that okay?"

I nod. "Yes, but I want a ring."

He laughs as he pulls me close. "I'll buy you the biggest diamond I can find."

I shake my head. "I don't want a big diamond. I want something simple but meaningful. Something that shows our love is real."

He kisses me gently. "I'll find the perfect ring for you, and I'll propose properly. I promise."

I kiss him back. "I'm holding you to that, Tillman." My hands slide down his body to cup his erection. "Now, stop talking and make love to me."

He growls as he lifts me onto the bed. "In the interest of full disclosure..."

I arch a brow as he gently lays me on my side. "Yes?"

"I've been fighting my feelings for you for a long time...even before you got pregnant. It was two Christmases ago when I looked across the room and really saw you for the first time, beyond our veneer of dislike and arguing. I was desperate to break through all that but didn't know how.

"Then I tried to forget it and return to the comfortable safety of being with Lara...but the thoughts and feelings lingered and grew. I knew I couldn't be with her anymore, but I didn't know how to tell her. You seemed to hate me, or at least barely tolerate me, so it felt futile."

I stare at him in shock for a long moment. "I had no idea. I can't pretend my feelings changed for you that far back, other than I realized you weren't the typical billionaire spoiled playboy I'd expected you to be. I was attracted to you, but I was determined to resist."

He slides into me, making me moan. "I'm glad you gave in. I'm glad we're here together, and you're having my baby. I'm grateful for the chance to be a father, and I'm thrilled to be with you."

I wrap my leg around his hip, drawing him in deeper. "I'm glad too. I love you, Maddox."

He starts to move, and I gasp as pleasure shoots through me. "I love you too, Jessica. I can't wait to spend the rest of my life with you and Charlotte."

"Me too." I cry out as he thrusts harder, and the pleasure builds. "Harder, Maddox. Please, harder."

He obliges, driving into me with powerful strokes that make me scream. "Is that good, baby?"

I nod frantically. "Yes, yes."

He reaches between us to stroke my clit, and I explode, coming so hard that I see stars. He keeps going, pushing me to another peak, and then he comes with a groan, filling me with his seed. The moment feels perfect, if a bit new and fragile. We're in love and committed to each other and our daughter. It's a dream come true, and I can't wait to see what the future brings.

WE SPEND THE NEXT MONTH strengthening our bond, and I'm low-key awaiting a proposal. I expect it to be in some elaborate restaurant, but he blindsides me one afternoon while walking through the park. We're strolling through the gardens, admiring the flowers, when he stops and turns to me.

"Jessica, will you marry me?" He drops to his knee and opens a box with a beautiful emerald-cut diamond in it.

I blink in surprise, glancing around at the people who have stopped to watch. I hadn't expected him to do it here, but it's perfect. He's perfect. "Of course, I will."

He slips the ring on my finger, and we embrace, kissing amidst cheers from the crowd. When we separate, he looks into my eyes. "I love you, and I can't wait to spend my life with you."

"I love you too, Maddox. I never imagined I could be this happy."

He kisses me again, and the crowd erupts into more applause. It's the beginning of our happily ever after, and I know we'll have many more moments like this one.

"When?" I ask when we finally pull away.

"I thought we could rent an island, get married there, and spend at least a month for our babymoon-slash-honeymoon. The sooner, the better."

I laugh. "I'm due in three months. I don't think that's soon enough."

"We can do it in two weeks. It's not like we have to plan much. We'll invite our friends, and we'll have a small ceremony on the beach." He grins. "I asked Willow, and she said as long as we get married within two weeks, you won't be on the bi-weekly visit plan before our honeymoon ends."

"You've been busy planning." I'm touched that he's so eager to marry me.

"I want to be with you, and I want to marry you as soon as possible. I want to have a wedding night with you, and I want to wake up beside you as my wife." He caresses my cheek. "I love you, and I want to start our lives together."

I lean into his touch. "I want that too, and I love you. Let's do it."

He kisses me again, and then we walk through the park, discussing plans for the wedding. We set a tentative date, and it should be easy to manage, since between us, we hardly have anyone to invite—just Embry and a few nurse friends from the OB floor for me, and Tanner and Lara for him. Maybe I should be irked by his ex-girlfriend coming to my wedding, but I don't feel at all threatened. I actually want to get to know her better, and this is my chance.

Chapter 14—Maddox

I RESENT THE TIME IT takes from planning and preparing for our trip, but when my father asks me to come by his office to sign the paperwork relinquishing my shares of his company, I make time. I want it all done and off my mind before I get married, especially since I won't be coming back to the city for a month.

His assistant nods to me as I pass her, and something in her worried look prepares me that things aren't as they seem. When I enter, I'm annoyed but not surprised to find my father and Lara's father standing together like a couple of vultures, circling prey.

"What is this?" I let the door close as I stride toward them. "Since when is Chester required for me to sign over my shares, Father?"

My father glares at me. "This isn't about that, Maddox. This is about you ruining your life and our family name. It's unacceptable, and we won't allow it."

I glance between them. "Allow it?" I glare at Chester. "What business is it of yours?" Not that it's my father's business either.

"Philip and I have to do what's best for our kids. You're the best thing for Lara. This rock star madness..." He shakes his head. "She's gone off the rails. She needs to be with you."

"She's not a child, Chester. She can make her own decisions." I turn to my father. "And why are you involved in this? Why are you siding with Chester?"

"Because he's right. Lara is the best thing for you. She's our kind of people and knows how to avoid embarrassing the family name. A few road bumps aside from both of you, we know we can count on you to fall in line and do what's right for our families."

I gape at them. "Our families? What the hell are you talking about?"

"Your marriage to Lara. It's the only solution. Your mother and I have already spoken to the Briggs, and they agree. Lara is the best choice for you, and they'll forgive you for the surrogate nonsense if you marry her."

"Marry her?" I can't believe my ears. "I'm marrying Jessica. We're getting married in a week, and nothing you say will change that. I'm not marrying Lara, and I'm not giving up my baby."

"Be reasonable," says Lara's father. "Our attorneys have drawn up an ironclad document. You sign it, the black girl signs it, and everything is handled. She gets enough money to give the child a lavish lifestyle, and you give up your rights. You and Lara can have more children."

I glare at Chester. "Lara doesn't want to have kids. Ever. With me or anyone else. I used to have that same view, and there's nothing wrong with it. We aren't getting married to each other, and there's nothing you can do to force us. I'm not signing anything."

"If you don't, we'll disinherit you. You'll lose everything, Maddox. The house, the trust, the cars, the jet, the stocks, and the shares. Everything. You'll be penniless and homeless, and you'll be lucky if we let you keep the job you have."

My father is so tone deaf. "I quit that job months ago, after Mother made it clear how little my grief mattered in the scheme of things...and for other reasons. I don't need any of those things, and might I remind you...Grandma Lucy left me a trust fund. I haven't touched the one from you and Mother, so yank it."

"You ungrateful little shit," spits my father. "Do you have any idea what we've sacrificed for you? How hard we've worked to give you a good life?"

"I know exactly what you've done for me, and it's not worth never seeing you or having a relationship with you to have the lifestyle I've had. Our family had an insane amount of money. You and Mother didn't have to work so hard to add to it. I wanted parents, not nannies, and I'll be damned if my daughter grows up without a father the way I did."

My father lunges forward, fist extended. Chester steps between us, and I shove past them both. "I'm leaving, and I'm not coming back. Don't try to contact me, either of you. I'm done."

"You'll regret this, Maddox. Mark my words," says Chester as I reach the door.

I turn to face him. "No, I won't, and I know Lara won't either. I just hope she can find a way to be happy too."

The two men stare at me in shock, and I leave, closing the door behind me. I'm free of the weight that's been dragging me down for years, and I'm ready to start living my life. I have a new family waiting for me, and I can't wait to begin.

I drive straight home and find Jessica in the kitchen, chopping vegetables. She smiles as I approach, and I sweep her into my arms, kissing her soundly. "Marry me tomorrow. I want to be your husband as soon as possible."

She laughs. "Tomorrow is too soon, but we'll be married next week." Then she turns to fully face me. "What's wrong?"

She can read me like a book, and I'm grateful for that connection even if I'm a bit unnerved. I never had that with Lara, for sure. "My father tried to get me to sign papers giving up my parental rights to Charlotte, and he also tried to convince me to marry Lara to save my inheritance."

Her eyes widen. "What? He should have known you wouldn't do that."

I'm speechless for me. Her absolute faith that I did the right thing is humbling. "Thank you. I didn't realize how much I needed to hear that until now."

"Hear what?" She tilts her head in confusion.

"That you believe in me. You didn't even ask if I signed. You just assumed I wouldn't."

She shrugs. "Why would I think otherwise? You love Charlotte, and you love me. There's no way you'd abandon us, not unless you were coerced in some way."

"They threatened to cut me off financially if I didn't sign and marry Lara. I told them to take it all, and they did."

"Oh, Maddox." She hugs me tightly. "I'm sorry they put you through that. It must have been awful. I have some money saved, and I'll be able to go back to work after our honeymoon as long as my placenta remains high."

I kiss her full on the lips. "You beautiful, wonderful woman. I have money from my grandmother. More than enough for the three of us...ten of us if we want a huge family, but thank you for jumping in, ready to make this work. I love you."

She looks almost sad. "I'm sorry no one has really believed in you before."

The words make me tremble. "That's not true. Holt did. And Anya...but you believing in me means the most. It's everything."

"I do believe in you. I know you'll be a great father, and I know you'll always be there for us. I also know that you're mine, and I love you more than I ever thought possible. I can't wait to marry you."

I kiss her again before the sizzling skillet gets our attention. "What are you making?"

"Chicken stir fry. Are you hungry?"

"Starving. I haven't eaten since breakfast."

She frowns. "It's almost six. You shouldn't skip meals. You'll get sick."

I smile at her concern. "You're going to be a great mother. I can't wait to see you with Charlotte. She's a very lucky baby to have you."

She beams. "I'm the lucky one. I have you and her. I have a family of my own, and I've never had that before except for Anya."

I hug her from behind as she cooks. "We're a family, and we always will be. I promise."

"I know. I love you, and I love that you want to marry me tomorrow."

"I wish it were possible."

"Me too, but I want our friends there, and I want to wear a pretty dress." She gasps. "I still have to go for the final fitting this afternoon."

I tug at her shirt. "Do you need help getting undressed to go?"

She laughs and playfully swats me. "Behave yourself for now, and you can have all you want later."

"I like the way you think." I kiss her neck. "Do you need a ride to the shop?"

"I was going to take a cab, but if you're offering, I'll take you up on it."

"I'm happy to. I'll enjoy watching you model the dress for me." I grin.

She shakes her head. "Absolutely not. You'll go get coffee or something. It's bad luck to see the dress before the wedding."

I pout. "Not even a peek?"

"Nope. No way. Now, set the table, will you?"

I kiss her cheek before moving to the cabinet to retrieve plates and glasses. "Fine, but I'm taking a bath with you later."

"Deal."

Chapter 15—Jessica

MADDOX DROPS ME AT the curb and goes to park in a nearby parking garage. We make plans to meet at the coffee shop across from the bridal shop when I'm finished, and I enter the store. Megan, the same clerk who helped me last time, smiles and greets me by name.

"How are you feeling?" she asks as she leads me to the dressing room.

"Great. I haven't had any issues since the placenta moved upward."

"Good. It's exciting that you're getting married so quickly. I'm jealous. I've been engaged for three years and still haven't planned my wedding."

I laugh. "I know what you mean. I was determined to be a career woman and never have kids, but I'm so glad I changed my mind. I can't imagine being without Charlotte now."

"She's a lucky baby. She has a great mom and dad." She gestures to the gown hanging on the wall. "Here it is. I think you're going to love it."

I gasp as she removes the plastic cover. "It's gorgeous." The satin and lace are stunning, and the empire waistline makes it perfect for a pregnant bride. "I can't believe I found this in the clearance rack."

"I know. It was a miracle. It's a discontinued style, but it's lovely."

I strip off my clothes and step into the dress. She buttons it in the back, and I stare at myself in the mirror. "I love it."

"You look amazing. It's going to be amazing with the veil."

I nod. "I think so too."

She helps me remove the dress and hangs it back on the hanger. "It looks like you're all set for your trip to the Bahamas." She sounds envious as she hands me my purse I dropped on the floor. Bending down can be a challenge some days.

"I am. I'm so excited. I've never been, and I can't wait to see where we're staying."

"I'm sure it will be fabulous. Enjoy every minute."

"I will." I'm passing over my credit card to pay the final payment, which includes alterations, when the bell on the door chimes discreetly. I look up out of habit but freeze at the sight of an older man in a nice suit standing in the doorway. He looks out of place.

"Are you looking for 'Edwin's Menswear?'" asks Megan, also clearly recognizing he doesn't belong there.

He scowls but doesn't answer her. He just bears down on me. "You're Jessica Malone."

My stomach knots with dread, but I try to maintain a cool expression. "I am."

"I'm Chester Briggs, and I'm here to deal with you. You can't be allowed to stand between my daughter and her happiness." As he speaks, he reaches into his pocket. From his dramatic phrasing, I'm expecting him to pull out a gun, but it's just a checkbook.

I breathe a sigh of relief as Megan reaches for the phone. He turns his head to glare at her. "Don't be absurd, girl. I'm not going to harm her. I'm here to enrich her life."

"Sir, I'm going to have to ask you to leave."

He ignores her. "Now, Ms. Malone, I'm prepared to write you a check for ten million to disappear. I have a document from Maddox relinquishing his parental rights—"

"You're lying. He'd never sign that." I angle up my chin.

"You're going to move to a nice, remote country, where no one will question the legality of the document. My jet is standing by to take you away."

I glare at him. "I'm not going anywhere with you. I'm marrying Maddox in a week, and there's nothing you can do to stop us."

"Ten million dollars could buy you a lot of freedom." He opens the checkbook.

"I don't want your money. I want Maddox, and I want our baby. I'm not leaving them, and I'm not going to let you bully me into doing something I don't want to do." I cross my arms over my chest.

He sighs. "Very well. I tried to do this the easy way, but you're forcing me to do it the hard way." He pulls out a syringe.

"What is that?" I back up but bump against the counter.

"A sedative. It's harmless to you and the baby, but it'll make it easier for me to transport you to my plane."

"You're not touching me with that thing. Get out," I yell, hoping someone hears me.

Megan is reaching for the phone again, and then Maddox is there. His roar of rage fills the shop as he rushes toward us, but I feel no fear. I'm not the one who's put him in this state.

Chester turns, and Maddox grabs him by the throat. "You bastard. You can't threaten the people I love and get away with it." He slams his fist into the older man's face.

Chester crumples to the floor, and Maddox stands over him, breathing heavily before he looks at Megan. "Please hang up. I'd prefer we handle this discreetly." With a cold smile, he bends down and retrieves Chester's checkbook. "How thoughtful. He'd already signed it."

He quickly fills in the information for the bridal shop and hands Megan a check for ten thousand. "This should cover any damages."

Her eyes widen, and she looks nervous. "He'll stop payment. He's a powerful man."

Maddox smirks. "No, he won't. He's not a fool. If he does, he'll be charged with attempted kidnapping, assault, and who knows what else. He'll be ruined, and he knows it."

Chester is coming to and clearly heard at least part of that. "You wouldn't dare."

Maddox kneels beside him, speaking in a low, threatening manner. "Try me, Briggs. See what happens."

Chester pales and nods. "I understand."

"Good." Maddox rises to his feet and extends his hand to me. "Shall we go?"

I nod and step over Chester, who's glaring at me. I pause and look down at him. "Even if you'd paid me off, Lara isn't going to marry Maddox. She doesn't love him. You should try supporting what she wants rather than hurting her by insisting on what you want. You're lucky to have a family, but you're driving her away."

He stares at me in shock.

"Come on, Jessica. Let's go home." Maddox wraps his arm around me.

I lean against him, holding my dress, as we walk out of the shop. "Thank you for responding so quickly. Did you see him come in?"

"No. I just had a sense you were in trouble. I'm glad I was right."

"So am I."

He kisses my forehead. "I'll always protect you and Charlotte. Always. I promise."

I smile. "I know you will. I trust you, Maddox, and I love you."

He grins. "I love you too. I can't wait to marry you."

"Neither can I."

"And I can't wait to take that dress off you with my teeth."

I laugh. "I was thinking the same thing about your suit."

He chuckles. "I guess we're both eager to get home."

"Yes, we are."

We hurry to his car and drive home, where we spend the rest of the evening in bed, though we don't involve our wedding finery. Yet.

THE FOLLOWING WEEK passes in a blur of activity as we prepare for our wedding day. We meet our friends at the private airstrip, where Tanner has graciously offered to let us all fly on his firm's dime. I notice he's flirting with Embry, and she seems smitten too. Love is in the air.

We have a pre-party on the jet, though I stick with sparkling cider. When we arrive on the island, the couple who acts as the caretakers for the enormous villa greets us, showing us our rooms. For this night, I'm bunking with Embry, though Maddox tries to convince me to eschew that tradition too.

"You're a terrible influence," I tell him as I hover on the steps, waiting to go up to bed several hours later.

"I'm a good influence. You just like being naughty."

"Maybe." I giggle as he kisses me. "Goodnight, Maddox. I'll see you at the altar."

He groans. "I hate to wait another moment to make you my wife."

"I know, but it's only a few more hours. Then you can have me forever."

"I can't wait."

I kiss him again and rush upstairs to get ready for bed. I'm excited and nervous, so sleep is a long time coming. Instead, Embry and I talk and laugh half the night before I finally fall asleep.

I wake early and find she is already awake. "Did you sleep okay?"

"Like a dream. This place is amazing. I can't believe how generous Tanner is to let us use it for free." She sighs, looking more smitten.

I laugh. "Maddox rented the villa, but it was generous of Tanner to volunteer his company's jet. I hope he doesn't get in trouble."

"I don't think he will. He's a junior partner, and he has a ton of vacation time. He said he hasn't taken a real vacation in five years."

"Wow. That's a long time. I'm glad he's finally taking a break. He deserves it."

"He does." She blushes. "I might sleep with him tonight, after your wedding, when I don't have a roommate."

I laugh. "Get some, girl."

She giggles. "I plan to."

We shower and have a quick breakfast before heading to the spa for massages and facials. Then we return to the villa, where a stylist and makeup artist await in the room, along with a light luncheon the caretakers laid out for the bridal party.

Suddenly, I'm acutely aware of Anya not being here, and I have to sit down as a wave of grief threatens to crush me. She should be here, laughing and joking with me, helping me get ready. "I miss Anya."

Embry sits beside me, her eyes filled with tears. "I wasn't as close to her, but I miss her too. She would have loved to be here today."

I nod and wipe my eyes. "I was at her wedding to Holt. The only person with any melanin in the entire church. It was like a sea of white, but they were so happy that I couldn't refuse to participate even if most of the people made me feel like I didn't belong. Not Anya though. She was my sister in all the important ways." My voice cracks. "She was supposed to be my matron-of-honor if I ever got married."

Embry hugs me. "I know. I'm sorry she's not here. I wish she were."

"Me too. I wish they both were."

She nods. "I know, but when you think about it...this wedding might not be happening if things hadn't unfolded as they did. You wouldn't be raising Charlotte, and you wouldn't have seen the side of Maddox that let you fall in love with him."

I sniffle and nod. "That's true. I'm grateful for the time I had with her, even if it was brief. She gave me the greatest gift anyone could give me."

"She did. And you're giving her daughter the best life possible. She would be proud of you."

"Thanks, Embry. I needed to hear that."

She smiles. "Anytime. Now, let's get you married. Anya would want that."

"She definitely would, and maybe she wouldn't be too shocked that I'm marrying Maddox. Or maybe she'd have lost her mind." With a sniffle and a small laugh, I rise to my feet and let the stylist and makeup artist get to work.

Two hours later, I'm dressed and ready to go. The dress fits perfectly, and I feel like a princess. Embry and I head downstairs, where the photographer is waiting to take pictures.

Tanner arrives first, escorting Embry down the aisle to the beachside gazebo where Maddox is waiting. He looks so handsome in his tailored linen suit, and I can't wait to get my hands on him.

Then it's my turn. I walk down the aisle alone since there's no one to give me away. I also don't have any attendants, because it feels better to have none than to have some but not Anya. Maddox waits alone too, for similar reasons.

When I reach the end of the makeshift aisle, he takes my hand, and the officiant smiles. "Dearly beloved, we are gathered here today to celebrate the union of Maddox Tillman and Jessica Malone in holy matrimony..."

As he continues, I lose track of his words and focus on Maddox's beautiful face. He's so handsome, and he's mine. Forever.

I say the vows when prompted, and Maddox does too. Then the officiant pronounces us husband and wife. "You may kiss the bride."

Maddox sweeps me into his arms and kisses me until I'm breathless. Our friends and family cheer, and then we head down the aisle, walking barefoot through the sand.

Once we get to the other side, we pose for more pictures. Then it's time for dinner. The food is delicious, and the wine flows freely, but I stick with water since I'm pregnant.

After dinner, the DJ announces it's time for the first dance. Maddox leads me to the dance floor and pulls me into his arms. "I love you, Jessica Tillman."

"I love you too, Maddox Tillman."

He spins me around the floor, and I laugh. "I had no idea you could dance like this."

"There's a lot you don't know about me, Mrs. Tillman, but I'm going to enjoy showing you."

I grin. "I can't wait."

We dance for a while longer before cutting the cake and feeding each other. Then we mingle with our guests, thanking them for coming.

Finally, we head to our suite, where Maddox carries me across the threshold. He sets me down and slowly unzips my dress, kissing every inch of skin as it's revealed.

"You're so beautiful," he says as he removes my bra.

I blush. "I'm huge."

"You're perfect." He kisses my belly. "You're carrying our child."

"I am." I run my fingers through his hair. "I love you, Maddox."

"I love you too, Jessica." He slides my panties down my legs and kneels to settle between my thighs.

I moan as his tongue finds my clit, and I arch against his mouth. He licks and sucks, bringing me to the edge of release and then backing off. I'm trembling with need when he finally lets me come, crying his name as the orgasm rocks me.

He moves up my body, kissing and caressing me as he goes. "I can't wait any longer to be inside you."

"I need you, husband."

He growls as he thrusts into me, filling me completely as he presses me against the wall. We don't even make it to the bed this first time as husband and wife. He drives in and out of me, making me cry out with pleasure as I cling to him. I'm so close again, and when he slips his hand between us, rubbing my clit, I explode. My channel tightens around his cock, and he comes with a shout, spilling himself deep inside me.

We collapse onto the bed, and he holds me in his arms. He's still semi-hard inside me, so I massage him with my inner walls, giving him a wicked smile. "Again?"

He groans. "Always." He rolls me on top of him and grips my hips as he thrusts up into me. "I can't get enough of you."

"I'll never have enough of you either." I ride him hard, chasing another release, and when I have it, he's right there with me in the release just like in life.

We're in this together, and he'll always be my rock.

Epilogue—Maddox

JESSICA IS BEAUTIFUL even in her suffering as she pushes to bring our daughter into the world. I wish I could take the pain for her, but her grip on my hand is giving me a tiny taste of it. I might need a cast when this is over, but I'm smart enough not to complain while she's squeezing out an entire little human.

"Push, Jessica," says Willow.

My wife bears down, pushing with everything she has, and then Charlotte is here. The first thing I notice is her shock of blonde hair. It genuinely startles me for a second, because I've sort of forgotten that Jessica isn't actually her biological mother.

The second is her ferocious wail, and I laugh in relief. "She's healthy."

Willow smiles at us. "She is. Do you want to cut the cord, Dad?"

"Absolutely." I take the scissors from her and sever the connection between Charlotte and Jessica, who collapses back on the bed as the nurses clean and weigh our daughter.

They wrap her in a blanket and put her in my arms. "Congratulations, Daddy."

I stare down at her, marveling at how tiny she is. "Hello, Charlotte. Welcome to the world."

She stares up at me with wide blue eyes, and I swear she recognizes me. She looks so much like Anya that it takes my breath for a moment, and I'm compelled to warn Jessica before handing her our daughter. "Prepare for the emotions," I whisper.

She laughs softly. "I'm prepared. It's okay, Maddox. It's not a bad thing to remember her. It makes me happy to see Anya's face in our daughter." Tears fill her eyes. "It hurts, but it's a good pain. A reminder. A blessing."

I nod and hand Charlotte to her. "I understand. I just wanted to prepare you."

"Thank you." She kisses the baby's forehead. "I love you, Charlotte. I love you so much."

I watch them, feeling like my heart could burst with joy. I never thought I'd have this, and now that I do, I can't imagine life without them.

Our baby yawns and closes her eyes, and I chuckle. "She's exhausted. I wonder if she knows she's been to the Bahamas and back."

"That's only one of the strange trips she's been on. Someday, we'll have to explain it all to her—why she doesn't look like me, and how much Holt and Anya loved her."

"I'm sure they would have loved her as much as we do." I kiss her forehead, incredibly grateful to have her as my wife and Charlotte as my child, though I'd bring back our friends to share this if I could.

But I can't, so I'll have to be content with the memories and cherish the time I have with Jessica and Charlotte. I vow to make the most of it and to never take a single moment for granted.

I have everything I could ever want, and I'm going to hold onto them with both hands.

Second Epilogue—Maddox

TWO YEARS LATER, WE'RE back in the same room in the same hospital, with Willow also in attendance of this birth. Charlotte is staying with Embry while Jessica gives birth to our son, and she's an impatient little miss to meet her baby brother. So am I, having been counting down the days—though probably not as eagerly as Jessica, who is tired of being pregnant.

"Why won't he come out?" she asks as she pushes through another contraction.

Willow chuckles. "He's not quite ready yet. He'll come when he's prepared."

"I hate you," Jessica tells her.

"I know. You must hate Maddox too right now, right?" asks the midwife with indulgence.

"Yes. He did this to me."

I shake my head. "I can't believe you're blaming me. It takes two to tango, sweetheart. Or in this case, make a baby."

She glares at me through the next contraction, and I wisely shut up. I know she doesn't mean it. She's in a lot of pain, and I can't blame her for wanting to lash out. I'm not offended, and I'll remind her of that when she's no longer in labor.

Finally, after what seems like an eternity, our son is born. He has dark hair, light brown skin, and dark eyes, and he looks nothing like Charlotte. I'm stunned by the difference, but I'm also pleased. I love seeing Jessica in his features and skin tone. He's the perfect combination of the two of us, and a symbol of our unity and love.

"He's beautiful," I tell her as I hold him in my arms.

"He's perfect," she says, smiling at me.

"What are we naming him?" I ask.

"I was thinking of Holt. What do you think?"

I slowly nod. "We'll have Charlotte Anya Tillman and Holt Tillman. What about a middle name?"

"I was thinking of your name."

I smile but shake my head. "No, I want him to have his own middle name. He's going to have enough to live up to with Holt." I kiss his cheek as she brings him to her breast. "What about Jesse?"

She frowns. "How is a version of my name his own name?"

It's my turn to frown. "True."

"Might I suggest Willow," says our midwife with a grin as she finishes delivering the placenta. She laughs a moment later. The two nurses throw in their names for suggestions too, but we're still trying to figure it out a few days later when we're home from the hospital.

I hold Charlotte's hand as Jessica holds Holt on her lap, ready to meet his big sister. She eyes him warily. "I thought we get puppy?"

I laugh. "No, a brother now, and a puppy in a couple of years."

She looks undecided for a moment before petting his thick dark curls. "Puppy."

I chuckle but don't argue as Jessica asks, "We thought you'd like to help give your little brother a middle name?"

I brace myself for her suggestion to be "Puppy", but she says, "Holt."

Jessica and I exchange a glance. "He can't be Holt Holt, can he?" Her lips twitch as she asks.

"Guess not." Her brow furrows as she thinks about it. "Holt...Wilson."

I frown. "Like that dog show you like?"

She beams and nods proudly.

I look at Anya, who's laughing, and shrug. "It's better than Puppy."

"So, it's settled. Holt Wilson Tillman," says Jessica.

"Welcome home, Holt," I say.

He stares up at me with those deep brown eyes, and I know he's going to have me wrapped around his finger just like his mother and big sister do.

I wouldn't have it any other way.

About Mia

THANK YOU FOR READING! I hope you enjoyed reading this book as much as I loved writing it!

If so, you might be interested in my reader club, where you'll get notice of new releases, specials, and other great goodies (like FREE books and FREE Chapters of upcoming releases).

As a special thank you, **you'll immediately get my book The Boardroom Connection, for FREE when you sign up.** No strings, you can unsubscribe anytime, and I promise I won't blow up your inbox.

What do you think?

YES – I'm in! I want to know the moment you drop a new release and get my FREE book! [Add Link: https://dl.bookfunnel.com/g14g65dcmd]

No, that's alright. I get enough emails, and I'll keep up with your new releases another way.

Again, I hope you enjoyed this book. You can learn more about my newest releases here: https://bwwmlovestories.com/latest-releases/ mia-latest/[1]

---

1. https://l.facebook.com/l.php?u=https%3A%2F%2Fbwwmlovestories.com%2Flatest-

releases%2Fmia-

latest%2F%3Ffbclid%3DIwZXh0bgNhZW0CMTAAAR34HFLR7qBe4ZmBHns_e4d0XgNz

eLpuTKitrQtc8gfqYam6Jwke4d05P5M_aem_AXZgxaooVqdkRI8v5k6ceTy7Gin_SGSOwZ0m

ohUpkMmzR-

Suzibzrob5LkW28qL53CXma0uvn_jG_N2FBJWICaiR&h=AT0CMUeqAaRQCxB-

vibJCLOB3BJo5qSFoE64VilifGretJ6ZtzkQOn3BhZ4e4cTX1Dpuw0RpYrElXkhsQlqHZNi1

DZdWlWOBOS2jn6YcuV5YinE0EhazJOy56rM3zQC4ziRiIOHCHTe8ohj45g&__tn__=-

And if you get a chance to drop a review or rating, I'd really appreciate it.

Best,

Mia

UK-

R&c%5b0%5d=AT06pfvEYO5wdSYGkilnE_RlU_XJQ3YtaKVXM3kw2RVJU7AEHMWZr

Kbz4ZVZ5KpHSvCa7Rpb3D9k4_NQuxDrhwHZHAVAvzrcdwCUjfoVuAu6L2M3OoNNZ

9qa849xyadSBygYxrAoFCijWjBix80lUGrim2l7h4DWuGnd8vRM3D-hcJAbp-

sg41WLy5X32P7Q

About Mylia

IF YOU WOULD LIKE TO be the first to hear about new releases, please join my mailing list[1] and receive a free book. I love to hear from readers, so please feel free to email me at authormashton@yahoo.com.

---

1. https://subscribeto.eo.page/myliaashton

Also by Mia Caldwell

International Billionaires
Her Grumpy Scottish Laird

The Brotherhood
Saved By The Master Sergeant
Sheltered By The Sergeant Major
Shielded By The Staff Sergeant
Safeguarded By The First Sergeant

Standalone
Marooned With The Billionaire Doctor
Enemies To Expecting
Ennemis En Attente
Feinde zu Erwartende

Also by Mylia Ashton

International Billionaires
Her Grumpy Scottish Laird

The Brotherhood
Saved By The Master Sergeant
Sheltered By The Sergeant Major
Shielded By The Staff Sergeant
Safeguarded By The First Sergeant

Standalone
Vegas Mistake
Marooned With The Billionaire Doctor
Enemies To Expecting
Cynthia And The Prince
Desperate Measures
Inferno